Laid I

Deep in stockbroker country, Thetfield was not on Inspector Angus Straun's list of golf clubs where the unusual might be expected to happen, so when on the 10th tee a player is killed by his opponent it seems at first to be no more than a tragic accident. But Straun is not convinced and probes suburban Thetfield's darker side. Why does a Dutch business tycoon choose a notorious confidence trickster as a playing partner? What prompts the thieves who raid the Pro's shop to take everything—including the waste paper? And how do golf balls come to be floating on the waters of a disused gravel pit? None of it makes sense until the scene widens to London and Angus Straun finds himself faced not only with murder but with what might well prove to be the most bizarre crime in the city's history.

BARRY CORK

Laid Dead

COLLINS, 8 GRAFTON STREET, LONDON W1

William Collins Sons & Co. Ltd
London · Glasgow · Sydney · Auckland
Toronto · Johannesburg

First published 1990
© Barry Cork 1990

British Library Cataloguing in Publication Data

Cork, Barry
  Laid dead.—(Crime Club)
  I. Title
  823'.914[F]

ISBN 0 00 232276 5

Photoset in Linotron Baskerville by
Rowland Phototypesetting Ltd
Bury St Edmunds, Suffolk
Printed in Great Britain by
William Collins Sons & Co. Ltd, Glasgow

For Alan Leslie
Companion of many a round

CHAPTER 1

As soon as I turned into Burbeck Gardens I could see that Angela's car was in the driveway of Aspen Cottage and I said rude things under my breath. Aspen Cottage belonged to her aunt, Molly Danby, the kind of elderly, amiable widow who twenty years ago had selected that name in cold blood for a neo-Georgian nest in Hampstead. By unspoken agreement it should have been Molly there to meet us, not Angela. Normally a considerate woman and not one to slip up on family protocol.

Sam said, 'Mummy's back.'

'Why, so she is.'

It had been my Sunday to have Sam. Or Sam to have me. Who has claim to who in the sad procession of fathers and sons by their one-time wives? An esoteric point which seemed not to worry Sam Straun, at six a cheerfully well-balanced child who seemed to accept having Dad one day a month as the natural order of things. Less than that when Angela was at home in Dorset instead of visiting in London, but he was a comfortingly normal small boy and resilient. He had a thing about gliding, so Laurie and I had taken him to Dunstable Downs, where people did just that.

'I bet you could hang-glide.'

I'd been lying on my back in the short grass, staring up at the multi-coloured wings hanging suspended overhead, knowing without looking up that my son had not been addressing me. Blood might be thicker than water, but for light conversation I'd suspected that Sam would choose Laurie's to mine any day.

From somewhere to the right of me I'd heard her mumble, 'No, thank you.'

'I bet you could fly a real plane.'

'I can fly a little one.'

I'd pushed myself up on my elbow. Laurie was stretched out a few feet away, a long line of check slacks topped by a yellow sweater, arms folded across her eyes, fair hair spilled against the grass. 'You never told me that.' She was my literary agent, a wingless species. More than my agent, come to that.

'You should know. No wonder you're such a rotten policeman.'

Sam, loyal son, had said quickly, 'Dad's a jolly good policeman!'

Laurie had smiled faintly. 'I was only pulling his leg.' She always spoke to Sam as though they were the same age.

'Why?'

'To stop him getting above himself. Isn't it time we were getting back?'

It had been time all right, but I'd wondered if she'd a point about getting above oneself. Sometimes I thought that life had been simpler when Laurie had been no more than my agent. And what was a copper doing with the arts, anyway?

I stopped at Aspen Cottage and swung in behind the parked Escort. By the time we'd got out Angela was at the door.

'Hello, Laurie. Nice to see you.' My ex-wife in a sort of green silk suit that went well with her eyes. Her dark hair was shorter than of yore and she looked fit and pleased with herself, which was somebody's doing, I had no doubt.

'Hi!' Laurie said. They got on well enough together, not meeting enough to discover much about each other.

'What did you do?'

'We went to Dunstable Downs,' Sam told his mother. 'Smashing.'

We went inside and Laurie allowed herself to be taken

upstairs by Sam to see some mechanical marvel, which was tactful of her but unnecessary. Angela took me into the living-room and waved towards a tray of drinks.

'A soft one,' I said. 'Tonic will do.'

She gave me a tonic in a glass packed with ice, American fashion, and looked past me at the Maserati sitting there with its red nose up the Escort's tail. 'I suppose even a policeman doesn't risk getting breathalyzed in a thing like that.' She frowned. 'You've changed it, haven't you?'

I said yes, I'd got rid of the Mistral. This one was a Khamsin.

'You do go for cars with odd names.'

'Maserati like calling their cars after winds.'

'Well, it looks very expensive,' Angela said, 'so I suppose the last epic went well.'

'Can't complain.' Indeed I could not. It was only my third book and the thing was selling all over the place. I had a sneaking feeling that Angela thought my indulgence in ludicrously costly Italian motor-cars was rather vulgar, but it was my only indulgence, so what the hell.

She smiled at me, matily enough. Our marriage had been something of a disaster but we'd emerged from the divorce still friends. 'I'm glad,' Angela said. 'I won't pretend I've read it, though. Blood and guts in mediæval England isn't quite my cup of tea. But I'm surprised you stick with the police when you could live in Italy or somewhere and just write.'

I said vaguely, 'Whole-time writing's a chancy business.'

'And you like being a copper.' Angela poured herself a second sherry, rare for her. 'You must be missing Harlington. Think they'll keep you in London permanently?'

'Depends how I make out.' Which was literally true, but I saw her looking at me curiously so I went on, 'They attached me to Bacton Road so they could assess my chances of getting back to the CID.'

'In spite of your arm?'

'It's better these days.' Marginally true, because old gunshot wounds don't usually improve with age, but I'd been lucky with a case and someone must have decided they owed me.

'I hope it works out all right,' Angela said. 'I mean it, Angus.'

'I know.' I watched her fiddle with her sherry glass, drain it and absent-mindedly fetch herself a refill. I wondered what was bothering her. Angela was no great drinker, but when she was worried the only thing she seemed to be able to do was fiddle with her hands. Fiddling at this moment consisted of filling a glass. 'Look,' I said, 'did you want to see me about something?'

She looked up at me quickly. There had always been a doe-like quality about those dark eyes of hers that I had once found irresistibly appealing. Maybe longer than once. It was all over and done with, but she had been half of my life for a long time. She put the glass down as though seeing it for the first time, perhaps knowing instinctively that she'd arrived at wherever it was she wanted to go and didn't need it any more. 'Why do you ask that?'

'You being here instead of Molly, for one thing.'

'God, am I as transparent as all that?' Angela dropped into a chair and shook her head in disbelief. 'I thought I was managing it all rather well.'

I said, 'Well, I know you rather well.'

'Yes, I'd rather forgotten that.' She paused. 'Angus, I do wish you'd sit down. You're off-putting, standing up there.'

I sat. 'Well?'

'It's nothing much, but there's something you could do for me for old times' sake.' She added quickly, 'Nothing embarrassing. But—do you still play golf?'

'On and off.'

'I've—a friend, who's mad about it.'

I said, 'If you want me to put him up for some club, he'll not get much choice. I'm only a member at Harlington these days.'

'No, it's not that. He's a member of Thetfield, as a matter of fact. That's pretty good, isn't it?'

'It's expensive.' Thetfield was a sought-after London suburb, full of stockbrokers and currency dealers. I'd played at the local club a couple of times and it was much as you'd expect. Not much on character but the best of everything.

'Well, that wouldn't worry Dirk.' If Angela had picked up a lack of enthusiasm for Thetfield, she chose to ignore it. She caught the query in my eye, though. 'Dirk Jager. He's Dutch.'

'They sometimes hold the Dutch Open at a place near Zandvoort,' I said. 'That's all I know about Dutch golf.'

'Dirk comes over here a lot on business,' Angela said. 'That's why he joined Thetfield. He's over here now, as a matter of fact. Only not on business. He's picking up his new Ferrari.'

'Angie,' I told her, 'people who come over here to pick up new Ferraris don't usually need much help from anyone.'

'Dirk doesn't need help—' Angela bit her lip. 'I'm sorry, Angus, but I'm doing this awfully badly.'

Policemen are trained in the craft of taking statements, more difficult than one might think. I said mildly, 'Tell me about Dirk. You say he's Dutch. Nice chap?'

'He is probably the most attractive man I've ever met.'

Point taken. Oh well. I said, 'You haven't answered my question.'

Angela frowned. 'Is he nice? Yes, I suppose so. He's sort of wholesome, the way Dutch people seem to be. Only a lot more high-powered.'

'So what does he do to make his money?'

'How do these people make their money?' Angela lifted her hands briefly. 'He buys and sells—property seems to

LAID DEAD

be his big thing. But he must be into just about everything, because he's really terribly well off. A millionaire over and over.'

'Made it himself?'

'He told me his father owned a barge.'

Did I sense a note of proprietorial pride? Well, why not? I asked, 'So what is it you want me to do for the man who has everything?'

Angela had a way of looking at one long and steadily when she had something important to say, a sort of sign that one could forget whatever had gone before but pay attention from now on, because this was the small print and you missed it at your peril. It was probably no more than a mannerism, unconscious even, but it was effective and she was looking at me fixedly now. 'I know it sounds crazy,' she said, 'but I want you to try and keep him out of trouble.'

I sipped tonic water and listened to the thumps and bumps echoing down from Sam's room, and I wondered what Laurie had let herself in for. I met Angela's troubled eyes again and said, 'Your friend doesn't sound as though he needs a minder.'

My ex-wife sighed. 'Well, yes. Dirk's terribly bright in some ways. Goodness knows, he must be or he wouldn't have made all that money. But in others he can be—oh, I don't know—unpredictable.' There was an expression in her eyes that I couldn't altogether place. It could hardly have been fear. Concern?

I asked, 'In what way unpredictable?'

'Oh, he's sort of up and down. He gets terrific enthusiasms and then gets furious if they don't work out. And it doesn't help that he can be so terribly—naïve.'

'Go on,' I said. 'Explain.'

Angela sighed. 'Well, he's always talking about this new friend of his—someone he plays golf with. I've never met him but it stands out a mile he's some kind of crook, a confidence trickster who's latched on to Dirk because he's rich and foreign. He's something to do with property and I just *know* he's trying to sell Dirk a pup.'

'Don't tell me,' I said. 'Tell Dirk.'

'My dear, he wouldn't pay the slightest attention.' Angela looked despairing. 'Dirk's the original MCP and he's convinced that when it comes to business, women should just keep their mouths shut. All the same, once the penny drops and Dirk finds he's been taken for a ride, I swear he'll go berserk. Frightful temper. He'll half-kill the wretched man and get thrown out of the club for hitting a fellow member or something.'

I thought it most unlikely. Still . . . I asked, 'What is it exactly that you want me to do?'

'Warn this bloody con man off. Tell him he's playing with fire.' Angela looked at me appealingly. 'You could do that for me, couldn't you?'

'Tell me,' I said, 'are you planning to marry this chap?'

'I don't know,' Angela confessed. 'He hasn't asked me.'

Which was honest, at any rate. I was not so much taken with the story as with the fact that I'd forgotten what a snob my ex-wife had always been. I'd always suspected that one of the reasons our marriage had broken down had been her dislike of being the wife of a policeman. It was entirely consistent that, while she'd thoroughly enjoy having a millionaire for a husband, he would have to be one who was socially acceptable. Being wife to a rich man who'd been chucked out of a smart golf club for ungentlemanly behaviour simply wasn't Angela's scene.

'Look,' I said, 'who is this menace you're so worried about?'

'His name's Wong,' Angela said. 'Freddy Wong.'

'Seriously?'

'Quite seriously. I've never met him but it seems he's half Chinese, half American.'

'Presumably,' I said, 'he's not short of a penny.'

'Loaded, I gather.'

'And you're scared that he is going to pull a fast one on your Mr Jager on club premises and the whole thing will blow up into a nasty brawl.' Put like that, it didn't sound very nice but then it wasn't meant to. Angela had no right to involve me in her sex life, as she very well knew.

She smiled ruefully and it prodded something that I was surprised was still there, but nine years is a fair time to live with another human being. When you're free, you think that's it, but bits of her have rubbed off on you, like it or not. She said, 'I'm sorry about this, Angus. I wouldn't ask, only I'm—well, in love with Dirk, I suppose.'

'I'll think about it,' I said.

I did most of the talking on the way home. It's not easy to explain to any woman why you're doing a favour for someone else, virtually impossible if one is telling one's present partner about something that has to be done for an ex-wife. Gifted with even a modicum of common sense, I'd have either announced simply what I was going to do or—by far the better choice—said nothing at all. As it was, I tried to justify myself and was making a sad job of it.

'The way I see it,' Laurie told me, 'is that you're going to make a fool of yourself, whatever you do. If you accuse Wong of being a con man too loudly, he'll sue you for slander, and if you try to warn Angela's Dutchman, he'll almost certainly tell you to mind your own business.'

'He may take a hint,' I said, but even to me I didn't sound very hopeful.

Laurie made a noise signifying disbelief. 'Not if he runs a Ferrari. He'll be long past taking hints from policemen on duty, let alone the ones who are trying to do it in their spare time.'

It was starting to rain. Not enough to be cleaned by the wipers but sufficient to spread the dirt on the windscreen to good effect.

I said, as though it was some kind of justification, 'Angela's in love with him.'

'Angela,' Laurie said briefly, 'is a bloody fool.'

Fair comment, that, I thought, and said without bitchery. There were times when Angela could be blind to everything except her own instincts, regardless of the fact that they were very often wrong, and this was one of them. So why go along with it? God knows the years with her hadn't been so good that the memory of them was a kind of bottomless deposit account on which she could draw at her pleasure. And yet . . .

Laurie's flat was in Kinnerton Street, off Hyde Park Corner, Bacton Street was only half a mile further on towards the Cromwell Road, so I headed that way.

'Please, Angus, not tonight.'

I said, 'I only want to call in the shop for a minute. Come on up if you like.'

She didn't answer so I switched on the radio. Outside the rain was coming down harder, and by the time we reached Bacton Street it was a steady downpour. Well, at least the afternoon had been fine for Sam, I thought. Look on the bright side, Inspector Straun. It is not your fault it is raining, nor that your ex-wife wishes you to save her lover from himself.

I pulled up outside Tiverton House. 'Well,' I said, 'are you coming up?'

Laurie shook her head. 'I'll wait.'

'I'm sorry about Angela,' I said. 'I didn't know she was going to be there. But she exists, just as Sam exists, and I like to see him whenever I get the chance. We three had a good day, I thought. We don't have to let this nonsense spoil it.'

'No,' Laurie said, 'we don't. Go on, then. Be as quick as you can.'

'So why not come up?'

'I'd rather listen to the radio.' She smiled to show that she really meant it, and I ran for the canopy in front of the entrance to Tiverton House. Not far, but far enough to get wet. Still, that was the least of my worries. I punched the lift buttons and sailed up to the lonely fifth floor.

Tiverton House had been built some time in the 'sixties as an extension to an extension of the Home Office, a bland steel and grass structure, much admired at the time by those who didn't work in it. These days it was an overflow for the Met, and Criminal Investigation shared the fifth and sixth floors with Photographic, War Duties and Accident Prevention. It had a slightly creepy air at weekends, not unlike a multi-storey car park in the early hours of the morning, only better lit. The duty staff shuffled about and spoke as though they were scared of being overheard.

I went to my own desk, which was exactly as I'd left it, and then had a word with the duty sergeant who seemed politely surprised that I'd come in at all and confirmed that there was nothing for me to fret over. Just as well, since I was preparing a working paper on urban terrorism.

'Hello, Angus. They repossessed your TV?' Inspector Thomas Broadbent of Fraud, two offices down the corridor, in his shirtsleeves, bearing files. Tom Broadbent, the finger of fate. Would he have passed by my desk had I not been sitting on it? Had I summoned him, or had he appeared solely by chance? I didn't know, but Tom was real enough and I knew that I was going to ask sooner or later, so why not now? I followed him into his office.

'Listen,' I said, 'have you ever heard of a half American, half Chinese character by the name of Freddy Wong?'

Tom Broadbent swivelled his chair round and looked at me. 'No personal knowledge, but something of a legend in the US, I believe. Haven't heard of him for some time.'

'You mean,' I said, 'that he really has got a record?' Bully for Angela and woman's intuition, I thought. It just went to show.

Broadbent said, 'Let's have a look.'

In the old days he'd have sat down cosily with albums of photographs, thumbed through dozens of card-index boxes. All changed. Broadbent sat himself down in front of his terminal and prodded at the keys, the kind of cop who'd taken to the microchip like a duck to water and always showed off his expertise. Now, as the keys rattled and the screen glowed green, the life and times of Wong F. began to unfold.

'So far as I remember,' Broadbent was saying, 'this Wong character has always managed to keep himself out of the slammer. Everyone knows he's one of the best con men in the business, but nobody's ever got around to making a charge stick. Probably because the marks won't press charges. Not surprising when you come to think of it— nobody enjoys admitting they've been had. Have a look for yourself.'

I had a look. Tom Broadbent's computer certainly seemed to know all about Wong, Frederick, born 1940 at Mineola, New York. Son of Janice Kaufman, singer, and James Wong, cook.

I said, 'How do you reckon they got together?'

'Could be they had a floor show at the Chinese takeaway,' Broadbent said. 'But don't let me stop you. Read on.'

I read on. There wasn't anything exceptional about Freddy Wong's early years, apart from the fact that he'd attended Mineola High, married young, divorced young and then volunteered for Viet Nam, where he'd won a medal for gallantry under fire. Discharged from the army in 1969 after a wound from mortar fragment. Worked as a salesman for an insurance firm before starting on his own as an 'adviser' in securities. From then on he seemed to have discovered his true calling. In 1975 he'd been charged with attempting to buy a fleet of cars on credit for a non-existent taxi business, but the case had been dropped through lack of evidence. In 1976 the St Louis police had tried to prove that he'd sold an ocean-going yacht that didn't belong to him, but they'd failed. They had also failed on two other occasions, on one of which Mr Wong was thought to have sold someone a diamond necklace that apparently didn't exist. The other had featured the rather ambitious selling of a private aircraft to its legal owner.

'How,' I asked Broadbent, 'did he get away with all this?'

'Dunno,' Broadbent said. 'Read on.'

I read on. By 1980 Mr Wong had left the United States and was trying his luck in Canada, and his luck had been very good indeed. There had been a hugely successful coup which had something to do with draining a lake, the details of which appeared to have been lost beneath a lot of official embarrassment, to say nothing of a contract for a phantom car rental fleet which brought about the resignation of a major government figure. By 1982 Wong had moved the base of his operations to Europe, where he had done quite well in Britain with a series of restrained but effective swindles which he presumably judged to be in keeping with local tastes. The following year he'd worked briskly for a while in France, selling rosettes for culinary excellence to greedy restaurateurs, after which he had apparently settled in Monaco for a period of recuperation.

To Broadbent I said, 'He must have needed a rest.'

'So did the French police, I imagine.' My man at the computer poked at a key, glanced at the lines of green print that came up and then turned them off. 'It goes on like that for quite a bit. Quicker if I tell you the rest.'

'You mean,' I said, 'he *doesn't* get caught?'

Broadbent smiled, sadly I thought. 'Not in this reel, he doesn't.' He swung round in his chair to face me. 'In 1988 Wong moved to the Middle East, presumably because he reckoned there was a lot of oil money there and he rather fancied himself conning some sheik out of a billion or so pounds' worth of crude.'

It was more than I'd have done in his place, and I said as much. Broadbent shrugged. 'Me likewise. But there's the compulsion bit. Freddy Wong couldn't possibly have needed the money. From all we know of him, he spends very little anyway, and apart from being a crook, no known vices. Which means that he went to the Arabs for the sheer challenge of the thing.'

I nodded, because it made a kind of sense. 'So what happened?'

'Frankly,' Broadbent said, 'we're not all that sure. But none of the Arab states love each other very much and you can always jump from one to the other. Apparently Freddy had an off day. For once he got himself in a bit of a hole. He had to find a refuge somewhere, so towards the end of '88 he became a resident of Jehar.'

I tried to sort that one out. Finally, I said, 'But isn't Jehar fundamentalist Moslem?'

'It is indeed.' Broadbent nodded his head in agreement. 'Freddy embraced the faith. He became a convert to Islam and a Jehari citizen.'

Well, it had a certain something. 'When you start conning the Almighty,' I said, 'you really are asking for trouble. But how come he's in this country?'

Broadbent said sourly, 'Better pickings, I suppose.'

I looked at the computer. Really, it was a bit of a nonsense, all this fuss about one bloody little con man. 'Fine,' I said, 'so the sooner we nick him the better.'

'You'll be lucky.' Broadbent stood up and stretched. 'We can't nick him. Ever. Because Freddy Wong is no longer a

con man. He's over here as Press Attaché to the Jehari
Embassy. And you can forget about nicking him. Mr F.
Wong enjoys diplomatic immunity.'

CHAPTER 2

I took myself to Thetfield the following Tuesday afternoon.
Not an altogether arbitrary choice of day, because I'd
checked with Angela as to when Dirk and his friend, Wong,
liked to play. Even so, it was still a matter of chance. I'd
toyed with the idea of getting the secretary to ease my
path but decided reluctantly that it wasn't on, favours to
policemen almost certainly running a very poor second to
the confidentiality of members.

'I hope you get thrown out on your ear,' Laurie had said.

I drove out decorously through London's suburbia, inner
to outer, and told myself that she could hardly be expected
to be enthusiastic about the project. Angela and I had been
legally married and just as legally divorced and that, Laurie
was entitled to think, was that, husbands having no business
doing favours for ex-wives, even for the most impeccable
motives. So why had I got myself involved? Because I was
intrigued by the inner workings of conmanship? Well, that
was one reason and a good one, although I had an uncomfortable suspicion that it wasn't the whole of the story.

Be honest, I told myself. Even if I didn't want to turn the
clock back so far as Angela was concerned, I didn't find it
easy to say 'no' to her either.

'Are you meeting someone, sir?' Thetfield might be exclusive but it liked money too, and the professional who
took my quite enormous green fee showed no desire to eject
me. According to the notice on the door, his name was
Bill Tilling (Assistant: Sandy Smith). He was well spoken,

good-looking in a film star of yesteryear way, well dressed and wearing rather incongruous gold-framed spectacles.

I said vaguely, 'I'm not sure.' I indicated his premises in general. 'Is Mr Jager here today?'

'Why, yes. Teed off about an hour ago with Mr Hunter.'

'Mr Wong?'

'I haven't seen him today, sir.'

Tilling was about to ask whose friend I was, so I changed the subject before he had the chance, which was a more than obvious ploy but the best available at the time.

'You carry a good stock, Mr Tilling. Do you mind if I have a look round?'

'Go ahead, sir. If there's anything you can't find, just shout.'

I went ahead, as invited. Back home at happy Harlington, Jack McCormick's lair usually offered half a dozen sets of this and that, a few windcheaters that didn't fit anyone and a rather sordid collection of second-hand putters. Jack was apt to point out that there was little point in laying out good money on stock when these days everyone bought their clubs from somewhere else at a discount, which was so obviously true that nobody had the guts to raise the subject any more. Thetfield members, I suspected, weren't interested in discounts, unless it was something worthwhile, like a few grand off a Cessna.

I walked round the shop for a few minutes, quite genuinely impressed. The place was twice as big as the usual pro's palace and there was precious little that the growing boy might want for Christmas that wasn't there. Matched sets of clubs seemed to stretch as far as the eye could see, studded shoes to equip an army. There were shiny fold-up golf trolleys and trolleys that plodded along by themselves on electric power. Rain gear, sun gear. Video equipment (*Examine your swing at leisure, complete with your professional's commentary and a full half-hour home lesson*). And if that wasn't enough, there were practice nets for your garden and—if you were really feeling rich—a selection of those little two-seater electric caddy cars so beloved of long course Californians. I couldn't begin to guess what it was all worth but presumably it sold or it wouldn't have been there. But I was impressed. Very impressed. Some places make you feel poor and this was one of them.

'Oh Bill, be a dear and fix this grip for me.'

This a well-kept lady of mature years with a club problem and, while Tilling attended to it, I drifted out into the sunshine and wondered what to do next. What had possessed me to pay a green fee when I hadn't anyone to play with? Because we are all creatures of impulse, that was why. Jager was here, just as Angela had said he'd be, but he was out on the course somewhere, in the middle of a game. And in the event that Freddy Wong was also here, how did I propose that we should meet?

I walked with bad grace in the direction of the club house, once a small Georgian manor. Not for Thetfield the clapboarded bungalow in need of a lick of paint. The place glowed in the afternoon sun and the Jaguars, Porsches and the Lord knows what else gleamed in the car park as their owners disported themselves over a hundred acres of immaculately maintained parkland. I don't know why I felt so tetchy about it all. Thetfield wasn't the kind of place that was full of inherited wealth, it was a safe bet that virtually every member had made his own pile. Nor were they more than usually revolting-looking people—most of the ones I'd seen were amiable enough looking souls. What troubled me was an uncomfortable sense of inadequacy brought on by allowing myself to get involved in something I should obviously have left alone. Moreover, Laurie had been quite right about this from the beginning and sooner or later I would have to tell her so.

I went up the steps into the clubhouse and located

the bar, empty save for a smallish, neat man in a long houndstooth hacking jacket standing with his back to me. He turned to see who'd come in and I got him full face. Just one more clean-shaven European, you'd say, only this one had a slightly olive complexion and eyes that slanted up slightly at the corners. Not displeasing, really.

'Hi!' said he, who could only be Freddy Wong.

'Good afternoon.' It made you humble sometimes. Fate. The unexpected sign of favour. And at least when you're looking for someone who's half Chinese, you know when you've found him.

'Can I get you something?' Freddy's clothes were so very much English that it was something of a shock to discover that his accent was American. Oriental eyes as dark as those of the chap at the Lotus House takeaway but with a good deal more humour in them.

'Coffee?' At that moment I could have done with a drink to celebrate, but perhaps not. He gave the order to the steward and then introduced himself with that engaging ease that comes so easily to his countrymen.

Freddy Wong. Angus Straun. Member? Yes—No. Good course but gets too crowded these days. The conventional chat appropriate to the situation. I drank my coffee and wondered what I thought I could do now. One could hardly warn a chap off in cold blood, quite apart from the fact that I was sitting opposite a legend. Every up and coming sleuth should add to his experience when and where he can, so I wanted to spin Mr Wong out a bit. But how? No trouble, as it turned out, because fate intervened a second time and generously arranged for me to drop my car keys.

It must have been fate because why else should I have dropped them, not being a fiddler by nature? But one moment I had them in my hand and the next they'd clattered to the floor.

'OK. I got them.' They'd fallen closer to Freddy Wong and he bent to pick them up. He didn't exactly do a double take over the key fob but there was enough pause to show that he'd taken in the red enamelled Maserati trident.

'The character I was due to play with let me down.' Wong handed my keys back. 'You free to have a round or you got something lined up?'

Exhibit surprise, mildly pleased. No more. 'I was planning on a few holes on my own, as a matter of fact.' Now the slightest hesitation, a qualm overcome. 'I'd be glad of the company.'

'Great!' Wong was studying me openly, which was to be expected from a man assessing an opponent's abilities, but the humour had gone from his eyes. Now they were blank —Chinese—inscrutable. My guess was that Freddy was not seeing me as a golfer at all, but as someone who owned a car that was expensive even by Thetfield standards. For a con man of his experience, that meant I was well worth three or four hours of his professional time. He asked, 'What do you play off?'

'Six.' It had been scratch in those happy, far-off days when I'd even managed to get through a couple of rounds of the Open, a handicap I was never likely to manage again, now that a bank robber's shotgun had made something of a mess of my right arm. But six shouldn't put him off, scratch might. I asked, 'You?'

'That's a funny thing. I shoot the same, so I guess we play level.'

I nodded. For a moment I'd wondered if he was going to claim a high handicap and then talk me into putting some money on the round, but I realized that would have been doing him an injustice. For one thing the bar steward was listening and would have a pretty good idea of every member's handicap, and for another, Freddy Wong was hardly the golfing equivalent of a railway card sharper. Yes, he was after my money, but he wasn't going to be satisfied with a paltry hundred pounds.

I got my gear out of the car. On the way to the locker-room my eye caught the handicap board and I paused to sneak a look, but nobody was pulling anybody's leg this afternoon. Wong F. undoubtedly was a member and, what was more, he played off six. Everything honest and above board.

'How come you're here this afternoon?' Freddy was in front of the locker-room mirror, straightening the collar of his Lacoste shirt. He was a snappy dresser, now in primrose linen slacks and matching cashmere. He sounded harmlessly chatty but he wanted to know all right.

I said, 'Curiosity. I played here once or twice years ago and I wondered if it had changed.'

'Has it?'

'No,' I told him, 'not that I can see.'

We made our way to the first tee amiably enough. I balked a bit at the caddy car my opponent insisted on hiring, but he was an American and presumably used to the things, and who was I to make trouble? We tossed for the honour and I won. I still wasn't all that sure what I hoped to achieve by all this but the sun was shining and nobody was going to question the fact that a round of golf was preferable to fooling around my desk at Bacton Street.

A suburban dream Thetfield may have been, but it didn't take me long to acknowledge that there was precious little wrong with it as a course. For anyone brought up on links, it would seem over-manicured, but by the standard of parkland clubs it was superb. At a guess, it had been laid out some time in the early 'thirties as a conversion from a private park. The trees that lined the fairways were no quick-growing conifers, dropped in by some contractor to break up the landscape. On the contrary, they were oak and beech, chestnut and larch—magnificently mature things that must have been there for anything up to a couple of hundred years. Artificial the lake may well have been, but like everything else it had been there a long time.

The first at Thetfield is a 375 yard par 4, almost dead straight but with a raised green formidably defended by no less than seven bunkers. You drive straight or meet trouble right away, because at one point the trees come in on both sides to form a kind of bottleneck through which you somehow have to thread your ball. It's a daunting beginning to a long eighteen holes and the bottleneck looks even narrower from the tee than it really is, and the good Lord knows that's narrow enough.

I drove and prayed. Someone up there in the great clubhouse in the sky must have heard me because I smacked it straight and true for what I guessed was about 220 yards.

'Great shot!' Freddy Wong said. 'Great shot!' He lined himself up. 'You want to have a little something on this?'

In a way I was disappointed. Puzzled, too. The classic card sharp makes his money by being an exceptionally good player who pretends to be a very bad one, thus encouraging his victim to increase his bet. But my handicap was a bit low for Freddy to try that—not unless he was at least capable of playing to scratch, in which case the club handicap committee would long ago have found him out. True, he could have changed a zero to a six on the board for my benefit, but in that case he would hardly have announced a false handicap in the hearing of the bar steward. I mean, how devious are you supposed to get?

I asked, 'What kind of a little something had you in mind?'

'Hell, I don't know.' Freddy Wong waggled the head of his driver reflectively. 'A three pack of Dunlops?'

That put me in my place all right. 'Fair enough,' I told him. Had he done that on purpose? Could be, could be not.

Freddy drove. He wasn't a man who carried a lot of weight but what he had he put into it, ending with the kind of long, high follow through that golf artists always draw in the How To Do It books. Most people with that kind of action have got it either through starting the game very young or spending a lot of money on the very best instruction. I watched his ball climb lazily up against the trees with just the right amount of fade and finally drop and run on to within a few yards of my own. Well, we were level on paper, and if one drive was anything to go by, we weren't far apart through the green, either. Golf brings out the best and worst in people. Could be the more self-respecting con men played it fair?

We ambled on. I felt vaguely embarrassed sitting in that absurd caddy car while Freddy drove, which was unnecessary because so far as most Thetfield members were concerned, it was the civilized way of getting round.

'Worse things to do than this,' said Freddy. Well, he was right. The sun worked its way through the trees and splashed dappled patterns of leaves and branches on the well-mown fairways and the wind blew a damp smell of loam and yesterday's rain. Half a dozen young rabbits worked their way unconcernedly through the short rough, miraculously unslain by the balls that thudded down around them. What with the trees and the occasional up and down, one played in a kind of pastoral seclusion, effectively hidden from whoever happened to be playing on the other holes. Idyllic, really, and remarkable for a club no more than a dozen miles from London, which, of course, was one of the things you paid for.

'A lot worse,' I agreed. We'd played three holes and he was one up, more by luck than good judgement, as Mr Aubrey might say. But I was enjoying the course and, to be fair, quite enjoying Mr Wong. He played sound, fast and highly competitive golf and his chat was brief, good-humoured and to the point—the kind of man who complemented rather than got in the way of the game. More to make some sort of conversation on my own account, I asked him how Thetfield compared with the clubs back home.

Freddy grinned. He had an engaging smile. 'Some better, some worse. The better ones I didn't get to join. You know something? In the land of the free a half-Chinese citizen in real estate has to box clever if he doesn't want to end up playing golf with a lot of other guys who are half and half. Now right here is where class is supposed to have grown up—right here in the United Kingdon. But you know something? Yours truly may run a chain of Chinese take-aways but I'm still an honest to God full member of this highly up-market club. So what do you make of that?'

I waited until I'd chipped over a bunker before I said, 'The committee would have to be out of its mind to blackball the owner of the local takeaway.'

'You're damn right it would. I'd make the bastards crawl for their spring rolls.'

Freddy had about forty yards to go to the pin and he laid his ball dead, not more than six inches short, with a sweet little pat with a 7 iron, which left me with a putt from the edge of the green for the hole. It was a long putt and I very nearly made it, but nearly is never enough. I gave Freddy his, which left him still one ahead.

I was beginning to think unkind thoughts about Angela. How was I supposed to tell this amiable character in cold blood that I Knew All and that he'd better forget whatever plans he had for conning my ex-wife's current boyfriend? Damn it, I quite liked the man.

I said, 'Have you always been in the food business?' No idle question. According to the computer, the nearest Freddy Wong had been to a restaurant chain had been when dandled on the knee of his cook father.

'No way. I'm strictly a real estate guy.' Freddy led the way to the 5th tee. He was telling the truth there, which was mildly surprising, if not disappointing. Why disappointing? I didn't want the man to be a villain, just one more crook for the book.

'So how did you get into takeaways?'

Freddy shook his head as I took a 3 wood out of my bag. 'You want to go short on this one, the greens raked like the side of a cliff.' Then: 'Oh, I had a deal with a coupla fellers who ran these takeaways. Wanted funding and I went in to help them out over a bad patch. The patch got worse, and in the end they ran for it, leaving me holding the hot end of the stick. So I been running it myself for kicks. Not bad, as it turned out. Lotta fun.'

I drove. Freddy drove. Into that whirring box and away. I said, 'So you're clobbered with it.'

He made 'yes—no' signs with his long, slender fingers. 'It pays,' he admitted. 'If you can get in, which is kind of hard. Strictly closed shop. You know where all the Indian takeaway people come from?'

'Yes,' I said, 'Sylhet.'

'Right! For Chinese takeaway, it has to be Hong Kong.'

'And you're not?' I knew he wasn't but there was no harm in asking.

Freddy said, 'Hell, no. I'm Mineola, Long Island. With a name like Wong, who cares?'

I played my shot. He'd been right about the club, and I made the green with enough backspin to pull the ball up dead. I waggled my club at Freddy in thanks. He duplicated my shot without difficulty and as we followed them up I said, 'So you've settled for a takeaway empire from now on?'

Freddy shook his head. 'I'm getting out while I've got the chance. Half-Chinese may be good enough for a while, but if I stay the Hong Kong boys will clobber me in the end.' He flicked the head off a daisy with his club as the caddy car whirred past. 'Got a deal all lined up. No problems. All I'll be left with is a membership of the Golf Club in far-off Japan.'

'The what?'

Freddy grinned. 'I thought that would throw you. But one of the things that fixed Lei On—the no-hoper who was losing his shirt on the Lotus House chain—was that he'd got ideas above his station. He was just crazy about golf.'

I said, 'You could say that about quite a lot of people.'

'Oh, sure.' Freddy nodded agreement. 'But this character was real wild. Used to play every day, which was how I met him. But seems he'd fixed himself a membership of this Jap club by doing a kind of deal second hand. Did you know you can transfer memberships in Japan? So I was going to throw the Tarasaka membership in with the deal, only the guy who's taking the takeaway chain off me doesn't play golf. Me, I don't see myself playing in the shadow of Fujiyama, so maybe you're interested? What do you reckon it's worth? Couple of cases of Scotch?'

I said, 'You'd be crazy to sell a membership of the Tarasaka for anything like that.' I'd met someone who had played there once, and his description had been graphic. 'It's one of the real prestige clubs of Japan.'

Freddy looked faintly surprised. 'So if it's a prestige club, how come they have a transferable membership? They could get *anybody* turning up. What would happen if Sunningdale was transferable and some member flogged his card to some crazy rock character with green hair?'

I said, 'They'd throw him out, but the Tarasaka is different, because just about everyone is golf mad in Japan and there just aren't enough clubs to go round. Chaps put their sons down for good ones just as people in this country used to order cars immediately after the war. In those days every car was in short supply. Dealers took years to fill your order, and when your number eventually came up you had to certify the car was for your own use. But apparently nobody paid much attention to that and you just flogged it at a hugely inflated price. If you put your name down for six cars, you got six profits. Same thing with golf clubs in Japan.'

'Then what's the going rate?'

I shook my head. 'I'm no expert. But the figure I seem to remember being quoted somewhere was around a million dollars.'

'Man,' Freddy said, 'you're having me on. Nobody pays that just to belong to a golf club!'

'For face or whatever,' I said, 'the Japanese will pay damn nearly anything.'

Freddy led the way to the green, twirling his putter reflectively. 'So you think I should keep the membership?'

'Well,' I said, 'in your place I certainly would.'

Freddy frowned in concentration. 'Worth thinking about. But like I said, not really my scene.' He looked up quickly as an idea seemed to strike him. 'Hell, it was your idea. How about you taking it off me?'

I lined up my putt, about fourteen feet with borrow to the left. 'How much?'

'Jeesus—I don't know!' I heard Freddy let out a long breath. 'You'd be standing to make a million bucks. Frankly, Angus—you mind if I call you Angus?'

'Feel free, Freddy,' I said.

'Well frankly, I feel you're way over the top on that figure, because even today and if you're right, a million is still one hell of a lot of dollars. Though half that is going on a fair day's wage—'

'So?' I don't normally go for rap putting but on this occasion I doubted my ability to stroke it firmly all the way through so I gave the ball a brisk smack and checked the club head at impact. It looked good from the beginning, though fast. I watched it rocket up to the hole, hit the back of the tin, leap at least a foot into the air and then drop back and vanish from sight. I straightened my back. 'How much?'

Freddy Wong rubbed his chin. 'British phlegm—I love it. You willed that shot in, you know that? You *willed* it in!'

'That's right,' I said. 'Steered it all the way. Now suppose you tell me how much?'

'Ten grand.'

I watched a black and white bird swoop from the trees beyond the green, closely followed by its mate. *One magpie sorrow, two magpies joy*. Well, it could be some sort of sign. I wondered how Freddy Wong had arrived at his figure. Ten thousand dollars for something worth in the region of a million was cheap—on the face of it too cheap. But one had to look at it from the punter's point of view. If Freddy really believed that the membership was worth all that money, he wouldn't be parting with it—period. If, as he said, he *didn't* believe the figure, ten thousand might be just about right.

'You on?' Freddy had his back to me, bent over his putt, which was shorter than mine had been, but no gimme.

'One of these days,' I said, 'you're going to try this lark on the wrong chap. Then you'll get a little note saying that you're not a member here any more.'

Freddy didn't alter his stance. I watched the head of his putter come back, then swing forward with a faint *click*. The ball ran straight and true. Went in. 'Halves,' he said. He retrieved his ball and turned towards me. 'What little lark?'

'Trying to sell me what is presumably a forged membership of a Japanese golf club.'

'Forged?' By this time we were deeply into the inscrutable Oriental bit.

I said, 'Since there really is a Tarasaka club and it's supposed to be pretty expensive, it seems likely that whatever piece of paper you've got is less than authentic.' I paused. 'That's fraud.'

Freddy smiled rather thinly. 'Listen, friend,' he said, 'I

don't know a lot about the laws of this country, but I don't reckon you're entitled to say that—'

'It's all right if you're a policeman,' I said. 'And I am.'

By rights Freddy should have either taken to his heels or said the equivalent of 'Orl right, guv, it's a fair cop.' What in fact he said was, 'It was your idea to sell the membership, not mine. It was *you* who said it was worth a million bucks.'

He was right, too. I found myself remembering something I'd read on the life and times of successful con men, and how much they relied on the natural greed of their victim. *You can't con an honest man.* But just the same I said, 'It won't wash, Freddy.'

He sighed. 'You going to book me?'

'What for?' I asked him. 'No witnesses. No money changed hands.'

Freddy raised an eyebrow. 'So you could have waited.'

'Look,' I said, 'I don't want to nick you. I'm not pretending your name doesn't come up in green lights every time anyone touches a computer but technically you're clean. You also play a good game of golf and it would be a pity to have to ask the Home Office to deport you. So I suggest you lay off. But for God's sake don't try your con game on fellow members, because they didn't make their money by being fools and it only needs one to complain and you're *out*.'

Freddy thought that one out for a while. Finally he asked, 'You on the level about this?'

'You keep your nose clean, no problem.'

'I appreciate.' I could see him appreciating it, just as I could also see him trying to work out what the catch was. He patted down a pitch mark with his toe. 'You're sure none of the members put you on to me? Jager maybe?'

I said, 'The members seem quite happy with you. And I've never met anyone called Jager.' The truth, so help me, nothing but the truth. I added, 'Who's he?'

'A Dutchman I play with sometimes.' Freddy paused. 'Should have played with him today but he called off. Said he'd got to play with some guy called Hunter, who was going to help him swing some business deal.'

We looked at each other. 'Well, if we're playing,' I told him, 'we may as well get on with it.'

He nodded. 'Thanks. Sure.' He led the way to the next tee and paused, frowning. 'Now what the hell's he driving up our fairway for?'

Good question. I studied the caddy car that was coming up the fairway straight towards us. Either the driver was lost or he made a habit of playing the course the wrong way round. I made get off the grass gestures but he came on regardless. Once abreast of us the thing stopped and a white-faced young man leaned out.

'Sorry about that but I've got to get back to the club house the quickest way. Get a doctor.' He gulped. 'I suppose you're not a doctor by any chance?'

I said, 'No. Why?'

'Something bloody awful's happened over on the tenth. Poor old Chris Hunter.'

Freddy spoke. 'What about Hunter?'

The boy in the caddy car drew a deep breath. 'He's dead. The—the chap he was playing with killed him.'

CHAPTER 3

Instil confidence, they tell you in the training manual; whatever the circumstance, keep calm yourself. No wonder there are jokes about Policeman Plod, the licking of the blunt pencil, the 'Now, sir, wot's all this 'ere?' But it works, nine times out of ten. It worked now.

'You mean there's been an accident?' Horrible murders

are rare on golf courses, although not exactly unknown. But the word 'accident' has a calming effect. It certainly pulled the lad in the caddy car up short.

'Well—yes.' I could see him sorting the thing out in his mind. Strange, the comfort of familiar things. Had he been reporting that a couple of cars had run into each other, he'd have been perfectly rational from the start. Now he said with something like relief, 'Hunter got in the way of his partner's swing. The club head caught him—here.' He touched his temple.

I said, 'You'd better see about that doctor.' It had happened before and would happen again, although most times it seemed to catch the victim in the eye. Not funny for Jager. And not a bit funny for Hunter, come to that.

'You think I should tell the police?'

'It's all right,' I said. 'I'm a police officer. I'll see to it.' It took a moment or so for the penny to drop, but drop it did and he sped into the distance at eight miles an hour. I turned to Freddy Wong to ask him the quickest way to the tenth but he was already ducking through the trees as though he knew where he was going, so I went with him.

We didn't have to go far. The tenth lay roughly parallel to the fifth, hidden by the intervening green belt. The tee was no more than fifty yards or so away, with two figures standing by a third that lay stretched flat on the ground. As we came up to them the younger of the two watchers said anxiously, 'Did you see Dickie? We sent him for a doctor.'

I said, 'He's on his way.' The speaker would be the youthful Dickie's playing partner, anonymously clean-cut and professionally promising. I turned my eyes to the other. Dirk Jager looked a pretty typical Class A Dutchman, fair, tough and wholesome-looking. The Dutch are a notoriously unostentatious race, socially conscious and liable to be upset by any suggestion that their crowded grey country is in any way tainted by divisions of class. Nevertheless, whether they like it or not, Dutchmen, like everyone else, come in different shapes and sizes, and Jager was quite clearly a product of the business end of the market, fortyish, fit and as tough as old boots. His eyes were grey and cold but no more than those of your average tycoon. There was something, though. A composure. A stillness. Perhaps the unimaginative Dutch didn't get into a state when they killed each other?

Jager nodded to my companion. 'Hello, Freddy. You heard what happened?' His English was clipped but almost faultless.

'We heard.' Freddy gestured to me. 'This is Angus Straun. He's a policeman. Too bad, I don't know his rank.'

I told him, and Jager turned those grey eyes of his on me. 'You got here quickly, Inspector.'

'I was here already,' I said. 'Strictly for the golf. Would you care to tell me what happened?'

He nodded towards the still figure. 'That's what happened. You want to take a look?'

No, I didn't want to, but life isn't a perpetual round of pleasure. I dropped down on my knees beside the unfortunate Hunter who'd been a sandy-haired, square-jawed man in his thirties who looked as though he might have been a good half back in his time. Now he just looked like someone who was dead, with a purple-black contusion on his left temple, from which a thin trickle of blood had oozed. I felt his heart and pulse, but there was no sign of life there and I stood up slowly. One never ceases to wonder at the sheer unpredictability of the human body, at the punishment it can absorb, the small things it finds fatal.

I said, 'What exactly happened?'

'I was driving.' Jager's voice was flat, matter of fact. 'He was hit by my backswing. I don't know how—I was looking at the ball. Perhaps he stood too close?'

It must have been a nasty moment, the feeling of your club head landing on something that shouldn't have been there. I looked up at Jager. 'He seems dead, I'm afraid.'

He nodded. 'So I thought. I have seen dead men before.'

Well, yes, he probably had. I nodded towards the body. 'You knew him well?'

Jager shook his head. 'Only as another club member.'

'Do you happen to know if he was married?'

'From something he said, I think he was divorced.'

Jager seemed to remember something and pulled off his nylon jacket and laid it over the dead man's head and shoulders. It was a natural enough courtesy and I don't know why it struck me as being a bit forced. For my benefit? I didn't know. Perhaps they did things differently in Holland. Then he said, 'I didn't quite catch your name, Inspector.'

'Straun.' But he'd caught it all right.

A lift of the eyebrows, indicating interest rather than vulgar curiosity. 'Then would you be—?'

'Yes,' I said.

'Ah.' Jager frowned at me and one got the impression that if he'd been paying my salary cheque it wouldn't have been a good time for me to take out a mortgage. He said, 'Something of a coincidence.'

Well, hardly a coincidence, considering the trouble I'd gone to to find him, but one couldn't put it quite like that. I said, 'I suppose the coincidence is that we both play golf.'

'True.' He looked in the direction of the clubhouse, from which a car was coming, driving straight down the middle of the fairway. 'That will be Dr Leigh-Smith. I noticed him on the practice ground this morning.' He looked back at me. 'All the emergency services to hand, so to speak.'

'Yes,' I agreed. 'In an unofficial capacity.'

It was a good line, so I used it when I rang through to
Tiverton House. It was a matter of routine to report where
I was and any kind of corpse lies uneasily on a policeman's
conscience.

'Unofficial capacity!' Superintendent Gareth Evans—my
Superintendent Gareth Evans—was not impressed. I could
see him raising his blue-chinned Celtic face and staring
accusingly at the telephone in his hand. The voice in my
ear said, 'Now suppose you tell me, boyo, just when you
consider yourself to be in this unofficial capacity?'

I said, 'When I haven't been assigned to an investigation
and when I'm playing golf.' I was still feeling my way in
unfamiliar surroundings and I might not have risked that
one face to face.

I could hear Evans Superintendent sigh. 'Point taken. So
you're out at Thetfield playing golf for pleasure, is it?' Pause.

'No,' I said. 'Not entirely for pleasure.' It was a temptation, but I could see the possibilities of getting uncomfortably bogged down in this one. Broadbent knew about my
interest in Dirk Jager and Freddy Wong, for a start, which
meant that sooner or later so would Taffy Evans. Oh well,
if you can't beat 'em, join 'em. I gave the sketchiest of
summaries of why I'd been playing that afternoon and
hoped for the best. After all, the afternoon had been owed
to me.

'Interesting,' Evens was saying. Another pause. 'A bit
different from what goes on in football clubs, see?'

I said, 'I don't know much about soccer.'

'Talking about football, I was, not soccer. What did the
doctor say?'

'That he was dead,' I said. 'It was about all he could say
until they have a post-mortem but he didn't seem to have
any doubts. In fact, he stuck his neck out far enough to say
that the inquest will be a formality. Accidental death.'

'And what do you think?'

A good question, because I was by no means sure of what I did think. I said, 'It's a fairly common sort of accident. You stand too near a chap when he's driving, and zonk—'

'So what is it you're worried about?'

'I suppose,' I said, 'because in most cases people get an eye knocked out. The angle of swing seems odd, somehow. Hunter's got a bruise smack on the side of his head as though the club was travelling almost parallel to the ground. Of course it might have been. Jager may just happen to swing like that. But there's something else—'

'Yes?'

'It's one of the first things you learn on the golf course—standing away from the man making a stroke. I had a look at the handicap board on the way in and apparently Jager plays to four, Hunter's handicap was nine. People who play to single figures don't usually make beginners' mistakes.'

'We all have our off days, boyo,' Gareth Evans said comfortingly. 'None of us is perfect, see?'

'True.'

'Are you golfers often murdering each other?'

I said, 'Not as often as rugby players.'

'Quick we are,' said the phone in my ear. 'But if you're feeling psychic you can be finding something out about this fellow Hunter. Married, was he?'

'Divorced, I gather.'

'Pity.' Pity he was divorced or pity there wasn't a handy widow around? One could never tell.

I said, 'The secretary can probably fill me in. But why the interest?'

'Not interest, boy. Routine only.'

'Well, it's hardly us, is it?' I said. 'Shall I get on to sub-division and let them take over?'

If there was a pause it was a very small one. Then, 'We'll tell them. You just carry on.'

Carry on, sergeant. Yours not to reason why. Just a small cog in a big wheel. Well, one might as well get on with it.

'Hunter, poor devil. What do you want me to tell you?'

The secretary at Thetfield was a neat, retired Wing Commander named Champion who didn't seem too happy talking about members alive or dead, which was not unreasonable.

'Well, his next of kin will have to be informed.' I imagined that would appeal to the services. 'Someone said he was divorced and hadn't any children. Still, perhaps his ex-wife—'

Champion seemed to have something else on his mind. 'Straun. Angus Straun. Didn't you used to play golf?'

'I've been playing today,' I said.

'I know. But you were in the Open once, at Muirfield. I remember seeing you there. You were the best amateur that year.'

'Yes,' I said. 'A long time ago.' In years it wasn't, but my serious golfing days seemed like something from way back.

'My dear chap,' Champion said, 'of course we'll do all we can to help you.'

'Just anything you happen to know,' I said. Just to be remembered is flattery, that insidious, guileful thing.

'His ex-wife married again as soon as the divorce was through and shot off to America. He divorced *her*, I believe, so there wasn't much joy.' The secretary looked apologetic. 'As a matter of fact, old boy, I distinctly remember Chris saying that, with Caroline gone—that was his wife—with her gone, he hadn't a relation to his name.' He thought that over. 'Of course everyone has *someone*. Fourth cousin second time removed—that sort of thing. But no one you could say he knew.'

'What did he do for a living?'

'Some kind of engineer. Clever sort of chap, I believe.'

'You mean,' I said, 'he had a garage? That kind of engineer?'

Champion looked slightly shocked.'Good Lord, no! He was something to do with dams and things. Big things!'

'A civil engineer?'

'Well, yes.' He looked relieved. 'A civil engineer. Did quite well, I'm told.'

'Then they'll have to find his second cousin,' I said, 'or the government will get the lot.'

It wasn't much but it was something to go home on. I had a so-called studio flat in Hallam Mews, but I stopped there only long enough to put the car away before catching a taxi for Kinnerton Street. I didn't expect to be greeted with any wild enthusiasm and in that, at least, I was right.

'There's an hour of daylight yet.' Laurie had answered the door but she stood at it hugging a manuscript to her chest, presumably to indicate that, so far as the evening's entertainment was concerned, she was provided for.

'I know,' I said.

'Do I assume that Mr Jager was taken queer?'

I said, 'Mr Jager is in the best of health, but yes, his friend dropped dead. Are you going to let me in?'

'I don't mind you being a policeman, and if I've got to hang about while you're serving society, so be it. But sitting darning socks while you run errands for your ex-wife isn't on, Angus.'

Laurie's eyes were troubled behind those huge glasses, and I'd have felt better about things if they'd been angry, there being a touch of masochism in the best of us. But she'd stepped aside to let me in.

I stood and looked at her. Since the advent of nylon there can be precious few women who have ever darned a sock, let alone stayed at home with a backlog of them, and Laurie Wilson was certainly not one of them, but then even I could see that these socks were metaphorical.

'You're right,' I said. 'Angela shouldn't have asked me and I shouldn't have gone.'

'Then why did you?'

I wanted to reach out for her but something told me she'd construe it as an attempt to evade the question, so I said, 'If you've been married to someone for a few years, you forget how to say no.'

'That came out pretty pat.'

'I'm not surprised,' I told her, 'because it's the same question I've been asking myself all day.' It may not have been the right answer but it was near enough and I pulled her towards me. The manuscript she was still holding was hard between us but her hair was soft and when she spoke her voice was muffled because her face was buried in my chest.

'You're a bastard, Angus. You know that?'

'Put your coat on and we'll go somewhere expensive to eat.'

I felt her brighten, even without seeing her expression. Like most women, Laurie was not greatly moved by food but addicted to going out inconveniently in order to eat it. But this time she changed her mind. 'I don't think I want to go out. I wouldn't mind some Chinese, as long as you get it.'

It rang some kind of bell from the last time we'd had a takeaway. I said, 'It's the Lotus House, isn't it?'

'I don't think I've ever noticed.' Laurie fetched the menu from its usual handy place behind the telephone. Surprising, when you come to think of it, that they don't make handsets with slots to hold things. 'Yes—you're right. THE LOTUS HOUSE AT HYDE PARK. I suppose that means there's a whole chain of them.'

'There is,' I said. 'And, what's more, they all belong to Freddy Wong. The chap I was playing with today.'

Laurie fetched me a drink. 'I thought perhaps you'd have been playing with Angela's Dutchman.'

'It's lucky I wasn't,' I told her. 'It was Dirk Jager who accidentally clouted his partner with his driver.'

'And killed him?'

'Yes.'

She was staring at me with a sort of fascination. 'I didn't realize you were serious. But Angus, that's absolutely awful.'

'It was for Chris Hunter,' I agreed. 'A cogent reminder to keep clear of the bloke who's hitting the ball.'

Laurie frowned. 'Don't be such a callous bastard. Doesn't it mean anything to you that this wretched whoever it was is dead?'

I said, 'Policemen aren't paid to be emotionally involved with crime, just to put it down.'

'Crime?'

'Accidents, too.'

We chose a meal and it wasn't until I'd fetched it and we were eating roast duck in peppers with water chestnuts that I started to laugh. I said, 'For a moment I was thinking that Freddy really did own the Lotus House chain.'

Laurie stared at me over a prawn ball. 'Well, doesn't he? I thought you said he did.'

'He *told* me he did. But that was when he was trying to sell me a Japanese golf club membership worth a million dollars.'

'He wasn't serious?'

'I should think he was exceptionally serious,' I said. 'Of course he changed his tune when I told him I was a copper, but up till then it was all systems go.'

'I wish you'd tell me exactly what happened this afternoon.'

I told her, and most of it sounded not unfunny. But Laurie

said, 'I still don't see how people like that earn a living. I mean, nobody in their right mind would buy a million pound golf life membership.'

'Oh yes they would.' I'd never had much to do with fraud directly but I'd read enough to believe that in the right circumstances a skilled con man could achieve anything. I said, 'There was a man named Morris who sold someone the Eiffel Tower. Twice, as a matter of fact, on the same afternoon.'

Laurie was making a neat pile of silver foil containers. 'I still don't get it. I mean, who'd *want* to buy the Eiffel Tower?'

'Well, scrap metal dealers would, for a start,' I told her. 'In fact, so far as I remember, one of the victims was just that. Morris told him that the Tower had been condemned as unsafe and that its remains were due to go to tender. He also claimed to be the government official whose job it was to arrange the sale. Said he was hard up, and for a consideration was prepared to see that the contract went a certain way. You see,' I said, 'the whole philosophy of the con is based on the premise that the punter isn't an entirely honest man. The real artist of fraud relies on his victim's greed and the fact that he's convinced he is going to get something to which he's not entitled. That's the theory, anyway.'

Laurie said, 'It sounds very cynical.'

'Well, yes,' I said, 'I suppose it is, but it must also have an element of fun. Challenge, anyway. There was a Spaniard back at the turn of the century who sold a battleship to a Quaker—a *Quaker*! And more recently a whole raft of tickets on the first space shuttle to the moon. There was a character not so long ago who made a packet selling off the Crown Jewels one by one, irrespective of the fact that the originals were actually on display at the time. But, of course, for the really successful operation you have to think big.'

'In other words,' Laurie said, 'the success rate varies as an inverse of the probability.'

'It most certainly does. If you tried to charge somebody five pence to use a free public loo, you'd be nicked in minutes.'

'And you think Freddy Wong will leave Dirk Jager alone now?'

I got to my feet. 'Well, he's no fool—he certainly won't work Thetfield again. I'll tell Angela the whole thing's a nonsense and to forget it.'

But it wasn't as easy to forget as all that. Later, as I lay in bed listening to the strange, three o'clock in the morning stillness when, for a brief hour, London traffic seems to stop, I wondered why I wasn't at ease with the day.

Beside me, Laurie stirred. 'What is it?' Did the quiet make it easier for thought transference? Or is there some kind of special sympathy people share after they've made love?

I said, 'I don't know why but something niggles at me. I suppose it's that chap Wong.'

'I thought you rather liked your Freddy Wong.'

'I do in a kind of fascinated way.' I turned on my side and looked down at the pale blur of her face in the faint light of the reflected moon. 'I just find it hard to believe in a half-American half-Chinese who's turned Mohammedan and works at the Jehari Embassy.'

Laurie laughed softly. 'I'm not surprised. The Embassy's only just been reopened, hasn't it?'

'Yes, we had too many shootings last time. We're getting a bit cautious about fundamentalist Islam.' I ran my finger round the faint outline of her jaw. 'I've never heard of anyone being actually slain by a golf club, either.'

'Does it worry you?'

'A little.' Or was it just the middle of the night? My great-aunt had had the Sight, so maybe I had, too. Or at least some residual, nagging left-over from it. I said, 'It's queer. I'm sorry for Hunter.'

'Both Hunters.'

'Both?'

'Jager means hunter in Dutch.'

'The devil it does!' I tried to see her face in the gloom. 'But you don't speak Dutch.'

'Yes, I do. My mother was Dutch.' Laurie put an arm round my shoulder. 'You got anything against Dutch women?'

'No.'

It was past seven before I next woke up. Laurie was still sleeping so I got out of bed carefully and went into the kitchen to make coffee. Out beyond the buildings on the far side of the little street the traffic was in good heart again, providing a steady background to the nattering sparrows brawling somewhere beneath the window. With luck, a nice day. I poured water into the coffee machine, found the filter papers and spooned in the Colombian before reaching for the wall phone. I should have left my number with the duty officer, but to ring up about midnight and say, 'Oh, sergeant, this is my number because I shan't be home tonight,' is rather asking for the old ho-ho.

'Straun here,' I said. 'Anything happening?'

Laurie had come out of the bedroom by the time I'd put down the phone. She had a towelling robe round her shoulders and looked about sixteen.

'Angus,' she said, 'you're not starting *already*—'

I poured two cups of coffee and fed one of them into her nerveless hands. 'Just checking.'

'I do hope something tremendously exciting's happened at the golf club.'

'Exciting, no,' I said. 'Odd, yes. Someone cleaned out the pro's shop during the night, lock, stock and barrel.'

Laurie's eyes opened wide. 'You're joking!'

'Well, that's what the desk sergeant said.'

'I bet the pro's mad.'

'I don't know if he is or not,' I said. 'And there's not much chance of asking him because he's not there and, what's more, nobody can find him.'

CHAPTER 4

So back to Thetfield, easier now that I knew the way but slower in the morning snarl-up. But at least drivers of Maseratis are excused the traffic lights' trial of strength on account of their holding a handicap of around plus 2. I took it easy and thought of Superintendent Gareth Evans and his whimsical decision to put the Case of the Missing Golf Clubs on my plate.

I'd said ineffectually, 'But sir, what about the local nick? Aren't they going to find it a bit odd if we come muscling in on some little local break-in?'

'Wheels within wheels, boyo. No objections there'll be, take my word on it.'

'Do I get to know what wheels?' He'd looked at me, so I'd added, 'If I'm supposed to be diplomatic it's best to know with what and to whom.'

Evans had looked disappointed. 'Nothing special, but both CID officers are members of Thetfield, see. Bit embarrassing having to poke around and ask questions of your pals.'

I reflected that in the old days Policeman Plod would have been lucky to have been offered half a pint round the back at Christmas, but at least it said something for the Thetfield members. Clearly law-abiding folk who had no objection to police officers being privy to their councils, which I suspected was more than the local tax inspector could say. 'Yes,' I said, 'I see. Anything else?'

'The Secretary mentioned you by name.'

The devil he did. 'He's an ex-Wing Co called Champion,' I said, 'but I only met the man yesterday.'

'Friend of the Deputy Commissioner, I hear.'

Well, there were worse places to investigate a breaking and entering and by chance my clubs were in the car.

'Have a drink, Inspector?'

'No, thank you, sir, not on duty.'

'How about a round when you're through?'

'Ho-ho-ho. Very nice, sir, I'm sure—'

The car park at Thetfield was fuller than I'd expected on a Monday morning, but a quick look round indicated that it was largely the veterans who were in full swing, grey-haired and cashmere cardiganed survivors of the City wars, but making up foursomes and doubtless planning to reach the turn just in time for an appropriate snifter, and very nice too. Not many women about, but I guessed they would appear after lunch. I walked across to the Secretary's office, narrowly avoiding a geriatric in a Bentley Turbo, and spotted a neat, newly lettered notice that read

> *Professional's Shop Closed*
> *Please pay Green fees to bar steward*

Well, someone had shown sense in shutting the place up. I put my head through the door of the Secretary's office and Champion waved me in.

'Glad to see you, Inspector. Makes it two days running, doesn't it? Hope you don't mind—'

I said I didn't mind and yes, I knew my way to the pro's shop. No need to trouble himself, and thanks all the same.

'The assistant is there, waiting for you. Sandy Smith.' Champion filled a pipe with the embarrassed concentration of a father explaining the facts of life. 'Bloody extraordinary thing for Tilling to do. Everybody liked him, you know.

First-class teacher and all that. Got himself into some kind of a jam, I suppose.'

I asked, 'How much was the stock worth?'

'I can't say off hand,' Champion confessed. 'A fair bit. But who's going to buy it off Tilling? Golf gear isn't like a load of cigarettes.'

'What makes you so sure,' I asked, 'that Tilling *did* take it?'

'We rang his home. According to his wife he's not been there all night, so presumably he's wherever the loot is.'

'Do you have his address?'

Champion scribbled it on a card. 'That's only a mile or so away, but if you want to speak to his wife, Winnie supervises the catering here.'

'How's she taking Tilling's disappearance?'

'Pretty well,' Champion said. 'She's good value, that girl. We get rabbits playing hell with our fairways—Winnie goes out most evenings and shoots a couple with a .22 Winchester she keeps in her office. Makes a good pie of them, too. She does a first-class job with overseeing the catering—very popular with the members. Obviously she's worried stiff— what wife wouldn't be? But she's doing her job as usual.'

'Good for her,' I said. 'But I'll have a look at the shop first.'

'Just as you please. The assistant will show you round, unless you'd like me—'

'No,' I told him, 'Sandy Smith will do fine.'

'Right.' Champion looked relieved. Well, partly relieved. 'You'll be getting tired of us. Interrupting your game yesterday over poor Hunter. Now this.'

'It's not your fault,' I said. 'It's just a job, you know.'

'Well—I did ask for you, as a matter of fact. Felt you'd be on familiar ground and that sort of thing.'

That was one way of looking at it, though, given the choice, I'd rather have kept golf and crime in two separate compartments. I said, 'It's an age of specialization.'

'That's what I keep telling people.' Champion looked cheered. 'Well, thanks again. Perhaps we might have a round some time.'

'Well, yes,' I said, 'I'd enjoy that.'

Sandy Smith was standing guard over the professional's shop as to the manner born, a chunky, red-haired young man with large hands who looked as though he was prepared to build a bridge or start a small war. I'd have thought that his future as a teacher was limited, but then, it's always been hard to assess these things. Anyway, I flashed my card and he sort of came to attention and let me in.

I said, 'This is how you found it?'

'Aye.' His accent was Lowland and faint at that. 'It was like it when I got here early on. The lock on the door was broken, you'll understand.'

I stood and looked around. Only yesterday and I'd been registering the place as one of the best stocked golf shops I could remember. Now it was no more than an empty shell, because whoever had been responsible for the break-in had done his job with almost ludicrous efficiency. I'd seen cases where the thieves seemed to have taken everything in sight, but rarely as thoroughly as this. Not only had the vast stock of golf clubs, sports clothing and general accessories been removed, but even the display stands had gone. In what had been Tilling's workshop there were four pale squares on the floor where the legs of his work bench had once stood, but of the bench itself there was no sign. The cupboards where he'd kept his tools had gone, along with the clock on the wall, the electric kettle with which he'd made his eleven o'clock cup of tea, and the waste-paper basket in which he'd dropped discarded grips. In the shop itself there were much larger light patterns where the dressing-out stands for the clothes had been, and raw screw holes in the walls where someone had removed the brackets that had held a mirror. Electric light-bulbs, advertisements and shelving had just disappeared, and someone had actually brushed the bare boards of the floor, leaving them unnaturally clean. It was as if someone had stuck the nozzle of a giant's vacuum cleaner through the window and simply sucked the whole lot up.

'They didn't leave much, I'm thinking,' Sandy Smith said.

'No.' I was studying the lock of the door, which had been forced, but neatly and with expertise. I asked Smith what time he'd got in.

'Eight o'clock. The course opens at eight-thirty.'

'Ever been broken into before?'

The assistant shook his head. 'No, sir, we have not. Not in my time, that is.'

'And how long is that?'

'A wee bit over two years.' And before that he'd been at Warton, a small club in Durham, where his father had been one of the groundsmen. Sandy had done a spell of that as well until he'd been caught by the urge to hit a ball himself. He was twenty-eight years old and could, he said, just about get round Thetfield in par. Unmarried, he lived in a bed-sit on the outskirts of the town.

'It's not much,' he told me, 'but it suits me fine, seeing as I spend most of my time up here anyway.'

I leaned against the bare wall and let him carry on. He seemed a nice lad who liked his job and clearly thought very little of anything else but golf. He liked and admired his boss and told me twice that in his opinion Bill Tilling was one of the finest teaching professionals around. The present whereabouts of that same Bill Tilling he considered as something totally unconnected with the sacking of his shop, a minor puzzlement that would be cleared up at any moment when the great man appeared.

'For a' anyone knows,' he told me earnestly, 'Mr Tilling's gone to see the doctor.'

'He might,' I agreed. 'Has he been feeling out of sorts?'

Sandy Smith shook his head. 'He didna say, and I'd not be asking, would I?'

'No,' I agreed, 'I suppose not.' I studied the position of the shop, the car park behind it and the long, low bulk of the club house. 'What time does this place shut up? Most nights. Last night.'

Smith said, 'The bar shuts at ten. There's not many here later than that.'

'And who sleeps on the premises?'

'There's only Jim and Doris Davis.' Smith caught my look of query and enlarged. 'He's the head steward and his wife's the cook. They've got a wee bungalow the other side of the club house.'

'How far the other side?'

Smith shrugged his shoulders. 'Fifty yards or so. It's away under the trees, near where they keep the gang mowers.'

Whoever had been collecting golf clubs must have had at least a van in which to carry his loot away, so why hadn't the Davis couple heard it? I went outside and remembered why: the Thetfield by-pass had an exit the other side of the car park hedge, which meant that even in the middle of the night there'd be the grind of articulated lorries heading for the motorway. A judiciously handled 2-tonner wasn't going to make much difference.

'Were those tracks here yesterday?' I asked. The drive from car park to shop looped itself round a spur of well-tended lawn, across which someone had rudely driven a heavy vehicle quite recently.

Sandy Smith blinked. Had the tracks been on the fairway, he'd have noticed them quick enough but lawns were not his problem. All the same, he said, 'No, sir, they were not.'

I nodded. There was a Nikon in the glove pocket of the Maserati, so I went to fetch it, tyre tracks having a knack of fading, which photographs do not. I was beginning to feel it all had the makings of a long morning, and I still had Bill Tilling's wife and Mr and Mrs Davis to go.

As sometimes happens when one's forebodings are at their worst, things went quicker than I had expected, although not necessarily better. Jim and Doris had seemed a straightforward enough couple, and their statement that they were both heavy sleepers and had heard absolutely nothing was going to be hard to disprove, even supposing they were lying, which I doubted. And Winnie Tilling? As I drove back to London I found myself thinking that Champion's description and my preconceived idea of what she was like had matched up. I'd pictured her as a brisk and efficient lass in her early thirties, dark haired, pleasant-looking rather than out-and-out pretty. So far as that went, I'd been spot on.

She'd said, 'No, Inspector, I don't know where Bill is. I haven't the faintest idea why he didn't come home last night. But whatever the reason, it's nothing to do with all that stuff being stolen from his shop.'

'Do you mind if I ask you a few questions?'

'No, of course not.'

I'd spent about half an hour in her little office, and as Champion had said, he girl was good value. I thought about what she'd told me most of the way back to Bacton Street, and even a worse than usual snarl-up of traffic on the A40 getting into Marylebone High Road did nothing to make her sound less convincing.

'God knows what's happened to Tilling,' I told Gareth Evans, 'but I think his wife's right. It doesn't make sense for him to have taken the stuff.'

'Why not? A lot of valuable gear you said it was.'

'Thousands of quids' worth, according to the Secretary,' I agreed. 'But I asked Winnie Tilling what her husband's job paid. Apparently he gets a retainer of five thousand a year from the club, plus his income from lessons and profits from the shop. On top of that he has contracts with a couple of manufacturers and some kind of interest in a driving range over at Hesleton. Taking it all into account, his job brings him in more than twenty grand a year. He'd have to be out of his mind to throw that lot overboard for a shopful of golf gear he'd find hard to get rid of.'

Gareth Evans rubbed his blue chin. 'You've a lot to learn, boy, if you think that. Plenty of men there are who've got good jobs and still need a few thousand pretty bad.'

'True,' I said, 'but his wife says she's got more than that in her own account. If he'd been in some kind of financial jam she could have baled him out.'

'Depends what kind of jam. Another woman, like as not,' Evans countered. '*Cherchez la femme*, as they say in Chapel.' I wondered if my superior officer had been a deacon, because he'd have made a good one.

I said, 'Not unless it's Rosa Constantine.'

'Speak on, Master Detective.' Powerful in prayer, we are, and patronizing with it.

I said, 'There were the tyre tracks of a load-carrier near the shop.' It had been quite an effort not to say, 'near the scene of the crime' but I made it. I went on, 'The tyre pattern was the same as the one we had for the Jacobson antiques job. It's a Ford Transit with two Firestones on the back and a Uniroyal and Pirelli mixture up front.'

'Owner Stephanos Constantine, known villain, who got off that one, with the help of a very dodgy alibi.' Gareth Evans should have been looking at me with new respect, but in fact he still seemed doubtful. 'Come now, Angus, you're *sure* it's the same?'

I said, 'I photographed the treads, if you want to wait till the film's processed. But it's the same mix all right.' I added, 'And the job's the same, too.'

'Total clear-out. Just like the moving men.' Evans was drawing something on his memo pad with a felt-tipped pen and I found myself studying it upside down. A building of some sort. For a wild moment I thought it might be a chapel but when he put in a lorry I realized he'd meant it to be Bill Tilling's shop all the time. He looked up and said, 'Do you want to go and have a look at Constantine?'

'Well,' I said, 'it wouldn't do any harm to see what his van was doing last night.'

Evans had started drawing a larger vehicle, this one had six wheels and a driver inside. 'Vans don't have a will of their own,' he reminded me. 'While you're at it you'd better find out what they were *both* doing.'

'Right,' I said.

'And leave us that film. A fallible thing is memory, see? Very fallible.'

Well, he had a point there, so I refreshed mine with the file on Constantine before setting out to meet him, for, as the man said, time spent in reconnaissance is never wasted. Stephanos Constantine was forty-two years old, born in Notting Hill, London, of Greek parents. After what appeared to have been a fairly normal childhood for the area, he'd taken to crime at the age of twenty-one and from then on had never looked back, or forward, depending on whose side you were on. He'd done two short terms of imprisonment for breaking and entering, both while under twenty-five, but from then on had managed to conduct a career of uninterrupted crime without the arm of the law cramping his style. If the various case notes were to be believed, this enviable state of affairs dated from his marriage to one Rosa Finch, the illegitimate daughter of a Berwick Market barrow boy, who was generally accepted as being the brains behind the Constantine team.

I took my treasures back to Kinnerton Street where Laurie was taking an afternoon at home, hoping to catch up on her backlog of client inspiration. She was hunched up at one end of the sofa with a dozen manuscripts stacked on the table beside her and I didn't help by reading out the juicy bits from the Constantine files, which was strictly against regulations.

'So what do they *do*?' Laurie demanded. She'd pretended not to be interested but after all it was better than fiction.

'You mean what kind of crime?' I thumbed through some of the pages, but that wasn't really necessary because Constantine and Rosa were part of my reintroduction to Criminal Investigation and I knew their story pretty well by heart. I said, 'They steal things. They're thieves.'

'Oh,' Laurie said. 'Is that all?'

'Well, they haven't been proved to have murdered anyone yet,' I told her.

'Then what makes them so interesting?'

I said, 'I suppose because they're specialists. The world's full of villains who'll turn their hand to anything but these two just enjoy knocking off premises in a wholesale way. They don't just take the odd choice piece—they drive up in a van and swipe the lot. They've done private houses so thoroughly that you'd think the place was up for sale. They empty shops. They drove off with the entire stock of a DIY store a few months ago and followed it up with a shopload of antiques belonging to someone called Jacobson in Camden Passage. Any moment now the south of England will be stiff with Black and Decker drills that fell off the back of a lorry.'

'There must be some nice little bargain antiques around, too.' Laurie's eyes had taken on a thoughtful look.

I said, 'There are never any bargain antiques.'

But she was interested, just the same. 'But seriously, if you know so much about them, how do they get away with it?'

It was a good question and one for which there wasn't any answer, apart from the genius of Rosa. 'She has a knack for arranging convincing proof that they were somewhere else at the time,' I told her. 'They never make a move without a faultless alibi. They're an extrovert pair. They even run a legitimate business called *C and R House Clearances*.'

'You mean they have a sense of humour?'

I said, 'It's one big laugh from morning till night, but it's Constantine and Rosa who do the laughing. I'd like to know how they're going to make money out of those golf clubs, though.'

Stephanos and Rosa Constantine lived in two of those mews cottages in Belgravia that are so highly sought after by the rich and famous. In Victorian times the carriage lived in the coach-house and the coachman occupied whatever space was left upstairs after the animals' feed had been stored away. During the 'twenties the pattern remained much the same, although it was the chauffeur who lived over the Rolls, until in the Noel Coward era a mews cottage became a fashionable home for the bright young things. Half a century on and with space at a premium, quite a number of owners who had spent several hundred thousand pounds on minimal accommodation had taken to turning their garages into extra living room. Rosa and Constantine on the other hand preferred to keep their cars under cover and made sure of adequate accommodation for themselves by simply buying two adjacent properties and knocking them into one. It must have been an expensive solution but, with business booming, undoubtedly the best.

The left-hand garage was open when I arrived at 24 and 25 Birkett Mews to find Stephanos Constantine blowing on the chromework of a sugar-pink Rolls. he was conservatively dressed in a Glenurquart check suit and suede ankle boots, and, both being of the best, they were kinder to the fuller figure than something off the peg might have been.

I said, 'Hello, Mr Constantine. Quite a colour you've got there.'

'It's a right bugger of a colour, as well you know, Inspector. But Rosa took a fancy to it and you know what women are.' Constantine gave his Spirit of Ecstasy a final polish and turned to welcome me. Seen from the front he had the blue-black hair and olive skin he'd presumably inherited from his father and the kind of rubber face that creased into a professionally engaging smile, but his eyes were like those of a shark, black and blank and utterly without compassion. The eyes of a man who'd sell not only his grandmother but his children too. They made the jollity slightly macabre.

'Rosa in?' There was little point in continuing the conversation if she wasn't, because without her Stephanos would simply play dumb.

'Rosa? In? 'Course she's in. Wouldn't let 'er out of my sight.' He glanced up at the window above him. 'ROSA!'

The window opened as if on cue and Mrs Constantine looked down. Bright yellow hair, hard china-blue eyes and a lot of red mouth, probably her husband's age, if not more. A small white poodle under her arm. She said affably, 'You don't have to bloody *shout*!' Then she saw me and smiled brightly. 'Hello, dear! What a nice surprise!' One could imagine her running a particularly vicious Victorian brothel. But bright. My God, she was bright!

I said, 'Hello, Rosa. All well with you?' As in Asia, greetings with the Constantines tended to be long-drawn-out but one ignored protocol at one's peril.

'All work and no bleeding play, but we mustn't grumble.' Mercifully the Constantines had not been blessed with issue or we should have been forced to go through their healths one by one. She exchanged a lightning wifely glance with her husband and presumably received some coded look in return, because she barely hesitated before saying to me, 'Want to come up, do you?'

'Just for a minute, Rosa, if you can spare the time.' Not for Birkett Mews the night-time knock on the door, the dread call of faceless men. Chapel Evans was all for the human touch, and why not?

'I'll lead the way, squire.'

I followed mine host upstairs to where his wife awaited us in a room that must have been an insurance assessor's nightmare, from Aubusson carpet, via various exquisite but unfussy pieces, to Lowry and Hockney on the wall. There was no point in getting excited about it because I was well aware that every item had been legally bought and paid for and that the bills were at hand to prove it.

'Do sit down,' Rosa said. She'd been at her best looking out of the window; the whole of her was too much like looking at a lady wrestler in pink diamanté stretch pants and a mohair sweater and lots of pearls. She said, 'I suppose it's no use asking if you'd like a drink?'

'I'm afraid not,' I said.

'On duty, eh, Squire?' Stephanos Constantine raised a large hand to punch me playfully, thought better of it and scratched his ear instead.

I said, 'I'm afraid so.'

'Have to be just Rosa and me, then. Oh well, first today.' He went to a galleried silver tray laden with this and that and sloshed gin into heavy cut-glass tumblers. Over his shoulder he asked conversationally, 'Are we nicked?'

'Now what would you be nicked for?' I did my best to sound pained. Nobody should say that Detective Inspector Straun lacked the light touch.

'Dunno.' He passed a glass to his wife and drank copiously from the other. 'You tell us.'

'Well,' I said, 'how's this for a start. Someone did over Thetfield Golf Club last night.'

Constantine raised dark eyebrows over the rim of his glass. 'Did they now. *Did* they?' He turned to his wife. 'Hear that, Rosa?'

'Bloody shame,' Rosa said. 'Lovely game, golf.'

In spite of myself, I asked, 'Do you play?'

But Rosa shook her head. 'No, 'fraid not. But we watch it on the telly.'

Her husband was eyeing me reproachfully. 'You don't think we'd have anything to do with a thing like that, do you, Inspector?'

'Well, you've cleared a few houses in your time,' I said, 'so I thought perhaps a golf club?'

'Cleared out proper, was it?'

'You could say that.' I paused. 'In a way it reminded me of the Jacobson break-in. The one you didn't do.'

'Funny about that.' Constantine looked genuinely puzzled. 'No doubt about those tyre tracks. Two Uniroyals, a Pirelli and a Firestone. Our van all right, wasn't it, Rosa?'

Rosa nodded. 'Yes, love. Our van all right.'

'Only, of course, it had been nicked. We was somewhere else, if you remember. We *proved* it.'

'You did indeed,' I said. 'By the way, where were you two last night?'

Stephanos looked vague. 'Dunno, squire. Can't remember. No, I tell a lie. We was in here, wasn't we, Rosa?'

Rosa finished her gin and fetched herself another one. 'Yes, love. Watching telly.'

'Not by yourselves, surely?' I said. Very few of the criminal classes watch television in the evenings without at least their solicitor and a couple of MPs to keep them company.

'No, we was by ourselves.' Stephanos frowned with concentration. 'Yeah, I remember now. Had a quiet night watching snooker. Enjoyed it, too.'

I wondered if they were going to pull the same thing twice, which seemed unlikely—certainly unlike the Constantines. But if they had no alibi for themselves they were going to need something quite startlingly probe-proof to account for the whereabouts of their van, which I knew was garaged at the S and R office in Ladbroke Terrace. I felt suddenly tired of playing pit-pat because it was getting late and I was planning to take Laurie out to dinner. 'All right,' I said, 'tell me about your van.'

Stephanos looked hurt. 'Our van? The Fordson?'

'That's it,' I said. 'The one that left its tyre prints across the grass at Thetfield Golf Club last night.'

Even Rosa looked hurt at that. 'Pull the other one, love. You know as well as we do where the van was last night. Or you should do.'

I shook my head. 'You tell me.'

Constantine sighed. 'Well, I got the bloody thing here somewhere.' He opened a drawer of a small Davenport and brought out a sheet of paper. 'Here, squire, look at this.'

It wasn't difficult to read because the type was a couple of inches deep.

This illegally parked vehicle has been immobilized
DO NOT ATTEMPT TO MOVE IT
It is an offence to interfere with a wheel clamp
Time: 1800 hrs. 5.4.89
This vehicle may be recovered from the Police pound
on payment of £30.00 plus £12 Parking Fee.

'Forty-two bloody quid,' Stephanos was saying in an aggrieved tone. 'An' I swear I'd only left it 'arf an hour.' He felt in his pocket and produced a smaller paper. 'Here —there's the receipt. Went down and picked it up after breakfast this morning.'

I glanced at the thing but it was all down in black and white. If the Constantines' van had been clamped at six in the evening and not reclaimed till almost ten o'clock on the following morning, it could hardly have been used to sack the Thetfield Golf Club. Not unless someone had found a way of unclamping it and then spiriting the whole thing out of the Police pound.

CHAPTER 5

It was odd meeting Angela again by assignment.

'I want to talk to you. Could you manage lunch tomorrow?'

'Why, Angus, how lovely! Just the two of us?'

'Yes, just the two. Webster's at one do you?'

'Of course! Just like old times.'

The stuff of farce, of angry wives and girlfriends locked in cupboards, Feydeau and Ben Travers. I wondered why it was I hadn't told Laurie. God knows, there was no reason why I should be furtive about seeing Angela, even if she was my ex-wife. There were questions that needed to be asked and this happened to be my case, but I knew very well that I wouldn't mention the meeting, because the experts say that it's only women who enjoy confrontations and, for once, the experts are right.

Spring had come to Soho as to everywhere else, warming the scruffy streets and putting some sort of gloss on the peepshows and porn shops amid which the district's handful of decent eating houses stood out disapprovingly like the richer half of an ill-matched wedding. At Webster's Angela was there waiting for me at what had been our usual table near the window on the second floor. She was wearing a hip length leather jacket over a cream woollen dress, her only ornament a necklace of some kind of Chinese beads of a red that matched the colour of her mouth. Her eyes welcomed me.

'You're not late,' she said. 'I'm early. You know me. Sorry.'

'I'd forgotten,' I said. But I hadn't forgotten the curious compulsion of that engaging woman. Angela couldn't help being early for appointments any more than other women could avoid being late. I told myself it was the time of year that made me momentarily hanker after times that were dead and gone. In the long run it hadn't worked. In the short term it had been sweet and wonderful and something to remember but in the end it's the long run that counts.

'Mr Straun, sir. And madam. A great pleasure to see you again.' Charlie, who'd always looked after us, smiling welcome, not a day older. But then, why should he be, we weren't ancient history yet.

I said, 'Hello, Charlie, good to see you too. We'll just have wine. A bottle of the usual.' I wondered if he knew that Angela and I were divorced. There was no reason why he should but there was precious little that a London waiter does not know, the odd fragments of other people's lives, picked up from here and there.

Charlie brought a bottle of the house white and he asked us if we would be eating the usual, too. We looked at the menu, with its endless permutations on a theme of fish, and said that we would.

'Crab pâté for madame,' Charlie informed his pad, 'followed by grilled sole for two, pommes sauté and leaf spinach. Only to start, sir, you will be having potted shrimps.'

We smiled and nodded, as pleased for him as for us, and considering the number of customers for whom he could do the same trick, it rated a round of applause. When Charlie had gone I said, 'How's Sam?'

'He's fine,' Angela said. 'He's adopted a frog.'

We talked about Sam and his frog until Charlie came back with the pâté and the shrimps. Then I said, 'It was unfortunate, that business at Thetfield yesterday.' I'd checked that she'd heard the news when I'd phoned her about lunch.

Angela said, 'I think it's perfectly horrible.' She knifed pale pink pâté on to a soldier of toast and then bit the soldier's head off with even white teeth. 'And what's this about a robbery?'

'Did Jager tell you about that?'

She shook her head. 'No, I read about it in the paper. Dirk phoned me yesterday, before it happened.'

'You didn't see him, then?' I said.

'He was going back to Holland last night. Seems that something unexpected turned up and he had to rush. He'll be coming back for the inquest, of course.' She looked at me. 'Angus, did you see it happen?'

'I was behind some trees on the next fairway,' I said. 'So far as I know there weren't any witnesses.'

'He must feel terrible.' Angela made a gesture of distaste. 'I mean, it was an *accident*—'

I said, 'Well, if he feels awful it's because it *was* an accident. If he'd meant to murder the chap he was playing with, presumably he'd be congratulating himself on a job well done.'

'You don't have to be professionally callous.'

I said, 'I'm sorry about Hunter, but accidents happen on the best of golf courses. What I wanted to ask you was: do you know what your friend Dirk was over here for?'

'Did you find out what this deal is with the Chinese man?'

'Not exactly. It's a bit more complicated than I thought.' I broke off while Charlie brought the soles, then picked it up again. 'Do you happen to know what Jager was over here for? What kind of business?'

I don't know what made me so inquisitive about Angela's Dutch friend. Absurd to suppose it could be some left-over twinge of possession. More a niggle of disquiet. Freddy Wong was a self-confessed con man, Dirk Jager some kind of legitimate businessman, supposing high commerce is ever that legitimate. Certainly they had nothing in common apart presumably from commercial rapacity, but I still wanted to know more.

Angela frowned. 'Dirk isn't the sort of man who talks business to women.' Then she shrugged her shoulders. 'Honestly, it's just as well because I wouldn't understand it if he did.'

I said, 'You said something about him picking up a Ferrari. Is he anything to do with cars?'

'Oh no.' She shook her head definitely at that one. 'He just likes them. But he says the Dutch aren't interested so he shops over here where people are a bit mad about the things. Probably just an excuse for a trip.'

'So he took one back with him last night?'

'Mm. So he said. But as far as I know, Dirk's business is property. You know—buying and selling.'

I didn't know but was trying to. 'What kind of property?' I asked. 'Houses?'

'Oh, goodness, I don't think so!' Angela sounded faintly shocked. 'Commercial property, I think. Office blocks— things like that.'

'Is that what he said?'

'He didn't *say* anything,' Angela confessed. 'It was just that sometimes we'd be going somewhere—round London, you know—and Dirk would say, "I just want to look at something." Then he'd stop in front of some buildings or other and stare at them for a while before he ringed them round in his book.'

Patiently I asked, 'What book? How do you mean, he ringed them round?' I asked people questions for a living and up till this moment I thought myself fairly good at it, but then I'd never had to interrogate Angela before.

'It was a big-scale road map of London, I think. Bound in blue and white. You used to have one like it, I think.'

'Yes,' I said, 'I still do. He marked the maps, you said.'

'That's right. He's got one of those fibre-tipped pens with red ink. Usually after he'd looked at one of these buildings he'd find where it was on the map and make a little circle round the spot.'

'But he didn't say why?'

Angela sighed. 'No, darling, he didn't say why. And I didn't ask because it was damn-all to do with me. And quite honestly I'm not sure that it's all that much to do with you.'

'Nor am I,' I told her, 'but you never know.'

We ate in silence for a time before Angela said, 'It'll be all right, won't it? About Dirk and this Wong, I mean. You won't let that little Chinese take him to the cleaners?'

'I don't think there's anything to worry about, you know.'

'Oh Angus, I hope not. But be tactful—Dirk's a bit touchy.'

'So am I,' I said. We rambled on through the meal but it was really a waste of time because, besotted though she was, the idiot girl knew practically nothing about Dirk Jager. I'd learned nothing, apart from the fact that he drew circles on a road map, and where did that get me?

'I'm sorry to disturb you, sir, but there's a telephone call for you.' Charlie, hovering apologetically. Webster's is all that it's cracked up to be but you may seek in vain for a telephone at your table, and no bad thing at that. But there was only one place that held my number this lunch-time.

When I got back Angela said, 'What's the matter?'

I'd have liked to have said nothing but it's not so easy when you've lived with someone for as long as I had with Angela because the giveaway signs are all there, flapping in the breeze. 'Sorry,' I told her. 'I'll have to go.'

'Trouble?'

'They think they've found Bill Tilling.'

'Oh, the missing professional.' Angela dabbed at her lips with a napkin. 'I wonder what he'll have to say for himself.'

I said, 'Precious little, I should imagine. They found him in a burnt-out car near Aylesbury.'

'You mean—?'

'Yes,' I said. 'That's exactly what I mean. He's dead.'

I've never liked the business of identifying a body. Someone has to do it but it seems barbaric to drag an unfortunate woman along to view what is left of her husband just because he happens to be the next of kin. But needs must and I drove over to Thetfield to give Winnie Tilling the bad news.

'There must be some mistake,' she said. The standard reply, alas so seldom justified. Man and woman's touching and unfounded belief that this awfulness cannot really be happening to them.

'Let's hope so,' I told her.

She looked out of the window. We were in her tiny office behind the bar, and outside, balanced on the branch of a lilac tree, a greenfinch was feeding one of its demanding young. It would have been easy to say that Winnie Tilling was unaware of the birds but that wouldn't have been true. She was seeing them all right, because she was giving them all the attention she could muster in a desperate effort to make them more real than the thing she was having to face. She was a tough, sensible girl and I imagined that she must have made Bill Tilling one hell of a good wife. I'd no idea what ups and downs they'd been through together but I got the impression that this wasn't the first kick in the teeth she'd had to face and she was coping the way she knew worked.

Finally she said, 'You don't really think there's been a mistake, do you?'

With someone like that you could only be honest. I said, 'I was talking to the Secretary. He happened to mention that your husband had had an accident to his foot. I circulated that along with his description, just in case.'

'And this—whoever it is?'

'There don't seem to be papers or anything like that,' I told her. At that moment it didn't seem necessary to add that the torso and everything on it had been so badly burned that there wasn't much left. 'But—yes. Whoever it is is missing two toes.'

She let out a sigh and looked at me. 'Well—that's that, then.'

'It could be a coincidence.'

Winnie shook her head. 'You're very kind, Mr Straun, but it isn't very likely, is it?'

I said gently, 'Frankly, no.'

'Better get going, then.'

It only took an hour to get to Aylesbury, and we didn't talk much on the way. We went first to the local nick and then to the hospital, where there was what the media like to call a considerable police presence, so I handed Winnie over to a WPC while I went inside to have a look.

'Did you know him?' a local Inspector asked as we approached the trolley with its covered figure.

I said, 'I met him once.'

'That's all right, then.' He took hold of the edge of the sheet and drew it back. 'His face is OK.'

Death does different things to different people, but to Bill Tilling it had been kind enough. It would be an exaggeration to say that his face looked peaceful but at least it showed no pain or fear or horror at what had happened to the rest of him. It was just still and slightly lead-coloured, the eyes shut, behind gold-framed spectacles that were still miraculously in place.

'Yes,' I said, 'that's Tilling.' I pulled back the rest of the sheet and wished I hadn't, because from the knees upwards the body was charred black. There was something more than usually nightmarish about that perfectly preserved head, legs and feet lying there attached to the calcined mess in the middle. The smell of formaldehyde or whatever was enough to knock down an elephant, but then they'd have to cover the other smell somehow. I retreated and breathed slow and steady. 'For God's sake,' I said, 'how did his face come to be left?'

The Inspector, whose name was Myers, shrugged his shoulders. 'Just one of those things. Freak of draught blew the flames off his face and legs and a lorry-driver chanced along with a big extinguisher before they got cooked along with the rest of him.' I discovered later that Myers worked in Traffic, where he had supped his fill of horrors, so it wasn't up to me to criticize the defence mechanism of a naturally sensitive man.

'Well, see his wife only gets the face,' I said. We went outside and I told the WPC to take Winnie in. I didn't look at her but felt her look at me. Her footsteps receded and for a moment I wondered if they'd stumble, but they didn't. A gutsy lady, Winnie Tilling.

'Anything else we can help you with?' Myers was asking.

'The car?'

'Two-year-old Granada, nicked from Henley last month.' Myers consulted a small notebook. 'F 43 YNG. Positively identified as the vehicle used in a warehouse break-in at Hatfield on the 17th of last week.'

I stood there and let that sink in. First Bill Tilling abandons a nice wife and well-paid job in order to steal a few thousand quids' worth of golf clubs. Then he dies at the wheel of a villain's getaway car. 'I suppose,' I said, 'there's no point in asking about the cause of death?'

'What do you think, chum?' Myers looked pained. 'The car was piled into a tree. Maybe the driver was tight at the time. Or had a heart attack. You'll just have to wait for the autopsy.'

'Yes,' I said. 'Sorry I spoke.'

The WPC was escorting Winnie out. They both looked pretty shaken, of the two the young policewoman the worst. But she was up to her job. I waited while she sat Winnie down in a car and one of the other officers got her a drop of something. I hung around a while and finally got in beside her.

'I'm sorry.'

She nodded quickly. It wasn't a time for luminous eyes shining with tears. Her face was blue-white with shock, shiny with sweat, but she drank what smelled like brandy from her paper cup and a tinge of colour began to show at the base of her nose. Suddenly she said in an unexpectedly loud voice, 'How did it happen?'

I said, 'We don't know yet. He seems to have driven into a tree.'

Winnie looked at me. '*Driven?* Bill couldn't have been driving.'

'I'm afraid he must have been,' I told her. 'There was nobody else in the car and Bill was behind the wheel when they got him out.' Then something in her manner got to me and I asked, 'What makes you so sure he wasn't driving?'

'His glasses,' Winnie said simply. 'He was wearing his glasses.'

'I know.' I remembered the curiously incongruous metal-framed spectacles on the dead face. 'But he did wear glasses, didn't he? He was wearing them the only time I met him.'

Winnie's hands were beginning to shake, so I took the cup from her and held them. 'He wore glasses for reading,' Winnie said. 'Bill was long-sighted. But he would never have worn them to drive with. He wouldn't have been able to see a thing.'

CHAPTER 6

'The Old Lags are due to visit Holland this week,' Gareth Evans, Superintendent, was telling the man from the Foreign Office. 'A bit of luck, that.'

'Old Lags?' The FO's man's name was Todhunter, forty-ish, brisk and wearing sandy hair and freckles on top of an appropriately expensive suit. He looked at me instead of my superior officer and raised his eyebrows. He could have asked Evans but perhaps that would have been too easy.

'Leisure Arts Group,' I told him. 'A kind of police eisteddfod.' Well, I could always write books for a living, which, come to think of it, was just as well if I was going to indulge myself with witty remarks like that. I looked past him through the window to where a squad of yellow-helmeted construction workers were demolishing the upper floors of an ageing office block and wondered if they went about their business the same way as we did. It seemed unlikely. A few Gareth Evanses among that lot and it would need more than those plastic crash helmets to save them.

'Joking, he is,' Evans told the Foreign Office. 'No eisteddfod at all. The Leisure Arts Group is a cultural society—very popular in the Division, too. Organized visits to opera, theatre and concerts they have, and trips to Europe if they can get enough members to make up a party. The present one is going to Amsterdam. Easy enough to get Straun here included in it.'

Todhunter said he thought that sounded an excellent idea.

'Wives go, too.' Evans was showing so much enthusiasm that I began to suspect he'd been a founder member. Then he must have remembered something he'd seen on my personal file, and looked uncomfortable. He added, 'Or friend, if possible.' He looked at me doubtfully.

'I suppose I could find a friend.'

He looked relieved. 'It's the cover you want, see?'

I said nothing, and Todhunter looked encouraging. 'You happy with the idea, Inspector?'

'Not altogether, sir.' The British reflex: peace at any price. Why was I incapable of simply saying 'No'?

'My dear chap, I can't see why. All very simple really. We have Dirk Jager, a respected Dutch man of affairs, keeping company with a notorious con man. For political reasons this is a most undesirable situation, so we are asking you people to have a word with our Dutchman and let him know the truth about Freddy Wong.'

I said, 'And I've been chosen to do the hint-dropping.'

Todhunter smiled. 'Why not, Inspector? You've met Wong. You've met Jager. I understand you play golf. All in all you seem ideally qualified for the job.'

Put like that he had a point. But—'To be frank,' I said, 'I don't see why I have to join this cultural outing. You say Jager is playing golf at his club for a few days. Why don't I just go there on my own?'

'A British policeman running about Holland on duty when he hasn't been invited would be most improper.' Todhunter looked quite shocked. 'A policeman who just happens to be in that country on an organized outing and who just happens to run across Jager on a golf course— *quite* another matter.'

It was my first experience of the delicate police – politics relationship and I wasn't impressed. In my book cops catch the robbers and nobody gets between them and their job. There shouldn't have been anything else to say, but of course, I managed to find something. 'What are the political reasons for wanting to keep Jager out of Wong's clutches?'

Out of the corner of my eye I could see Gareth Evans looking like a mum whose child has said something unfortunate at a party, because one wasn't supposed to ask questions of the FO.

Nevertheless, Todhunter replied easily enough. 'Jager has a significant holding in a British consortium operating in the Middle East. At the moment there's a very large investment at stake in a country—' Todhunter paused and then continued diplomatically—'in a country adjacent to Jehar, and the Jeharis are by no means happy about it. It's an open secret that they'd like to scupper the deal, and from what's known of Mr Wong, it suggests he's just the man to do it.'

'He probably is,' I agreed. 'But we don't know that he's not just selling Jager shares in a non-existent gold mine. I know he's technically a Jehari citizen but I'm sure that's simply a matter of convenience so far as he's concerned.'

'But his diplomatic immunity is still genuine enough.' Todhunter tweaked the crease of his trousers. 'We're trying to improve our relations with Jehar, Inspector, although God knows it isn't easy. Still, so far as Wong himself is concerned, you're to lay off. Far better to tip off the Dutchman. Once he hears that Wong has a record, he'll be off like a scalded stoat.'

'Freddy Wong hasn't *got* a record.'

Todhunter sighed. 'Well—you know what I mean. Just tell Jager how the bloody man makes his living.'

'As you wish,' I said. 'But I still don't understand why it wouldn't be a whole lot easier if we had a word with the Dutch police and let them pass the news on to Jager. Surely that would be official enough?'

'But you must know the Dutch are already touchy about Jager coming in on a British consortium,' Todhunter said severely. 'They'd *pay* to see Wong sink his teeth into him. Really, Inspector, do try to be sensible.'

I'd meant to take Laurie out to dinner but I think she sensed my heart wasn't in it and we ate baked beans at Kinnerton Street instead, while she asked me about the Old Lags.

'So how long have you been a leisure artist?'

'About a couple of hours,' I told her. 'It's not like a cinema club. You can get in right away.'

'And all these artistic policemen do is play golf?'

I said patiently, 'You're forgetting the art. Them as feels like it go to the Rijksmuseum for the "Night Watch". Some paint canals. Some play golf. It's a free and easy kind of society. Everyone follows his own star.'

She frowned and I waited. She was good with Sam, good at her job as a literary agent and, God help us, good with me. There were times when I'd been amused by what I was pleased to consider her assumed toughness, an acquired public front. With her mane of blonde hair and those periwinkle-blue eyes enlarged by absurdly large glasses, Laurie looked not unlike the young Bette Davis in *Now Voyager*, just waiting for that historic bit of old Hollywood when Paul Henreid sticks a ready-lit cigarette in her mouth and gently takes the damn things off. But looks apart, she was one of the three best literary agents in London, and when it came to doing a deal, tough as old boots.

Finally she said, 'I thought you were supposed to be coping with the Bill Tilling business.'

'I am. This Dutch jaunt is only for the weekend. More to the point is: are you coming with me?'

I think she really was surprised at that one. 'What on earth for?'

'Cover it is, boyo,' I told her. 'Most of the chaps take their wives—or friends.' I added, 'It could be fun.'

Laurie thought it over. 'I've got manuscripts to read. You know I never get time at the office.'

'I'm taking the car. Read a couple on the ferry.' Like all her craft, she read page by page, not line by line, no word missed as she flicked the sheets of A4 over like a teller counting banknotes.

'I suppose I could.' Her face lit suddenly, like a small girl given a present. 'I haven't been to Holland for so long.'

'I drove through it once.' Even that was a blurred kind of memory. A grey, flat land that had reminded me of the fen country.

Laurie said absently, 'My mother was Dutch.'

'I know. You told me last night.' That would explain

her colouring, I supposed. Did Ditch girls come slim and long-legged? I doubted it. Perhaps she'd inherited those from her father. 'You said you could speak it, too.'

She laughed. '*Ja, mijnheer. Ik spreek Nederlandser, naturlijk.*'

'That'll come in useful.'

She shrugged. 'Almost everyone speaks English these days—the films and television aren't even dubbed. I'd probably have forgotten most of it if I didn't use it over the phone to our Dutch associates.'

'I didn't even know you had such a thing.'

She said with a touch of exasperation, 'You got a cheque for Dutch rights of your last book quite recently. Who do you think negotiated it?'

I said, 'I didn't think.'

'The Dutch buy proportionately more magazines than any other country in Europe. Printing's a major industry. Rotterdam—'

'I take your point.' An idea had struck me. 'What's the name of your associate in Amsterdam?'

Laurie looked at me curiously. 'Seltje Brinmaker. Why?'

'I want you to pay her a call.'

'And?'

'She'll have access to a cuttings library, I imagine. Ask her to see what they've got on Dirk Jager.'

Laurie frowned. 'He's a big man in Holland. They'll have masses.'

'Just the juicy bits.'

CHAPTER 7

Between the port of Vlissingen and the seaside town of Zandvoort the country is as flat as your hand. Inland the fields stretch to the horizon under rain-filled skies, and the

barns and cattle look as though someone has scattered a
few toys around in order to break up the landscape. West-
wards there are holiday chalets and sand dunes and the
grey North Sea and through the windscreen stretches the
road. The Dutch build roads with the same uncompromising
efficiency they give to canals and the E47 is a straight,
superbly engineered highway, full of sensible diesel Mer-
cedes and VWs and restricted to a limit of 100 kilometres
per hour. In Holland most people behave themselves auto-
matically, but just in case, the police patrol in white Porsche
911s and are renowned for their lack of humour, so I kept
the Maserati in the inside lane and watched my p's and q's.

Laurie was on her way to Amsterdam by train.

'You'll pick me up Sunday evening?' She hadn't been all
that enthusiastic about the new arrangement but took it
without any real objections, by which I assumed she wasn't
all that averse to a couple of days in a city she knew well.

'You've got a note of the hotel?' How quickly women
assume their proprietary role, their guardianship of the
male. The hotel was thrown in with the trip, there were at
least half a dozen police couples who'd been on the same
ferry and were all heading for the same place. Laurie, my
love, I gave you the name of the hotel in the first place, I
am hardly likely to have forgotten it already.

I'd said, 'I've got a note of the hotel. If I get through with
Jager earlier, I'll let you know.'

She'd pulled at my jacket. 'Take care now.'

'I wasn't planning anything adventurous.'

I wasn't planning anything other than a quiet word that
could well have been delivered by someone else. I wondered
what had really happened to Bill Tilling. That Stephanos
Constantine had cleaned out the golf shop I was prepared
to go along with, although I'd have imagined him using his
doubtful talents somewhere more profitable. But that Tilling
would have joined in the project seemed unlikely in the

extreme. But then so much crime was just that. After all, if it was predictable the whole thing would be too easy.

A red Ferrari Mondial went past me with a glorious blast of sound, flicked neatly between a frozen meat truck and a tanker and then squirted away in the outside lane as though we were all standing still. Some 100 k.p.h., I thought, and wondered how far he was likely to get. I glanced in the mirror, half expecting to see a white Porsche already in pursuit, but there was only a scattering of practical square family cars going about their practical square business. I guessed that the Ferrari must have belonged to Jager en route for Zandvoort too. After all, how many Ferrari Mondials on Dutch plates were there likely to be?

Zandvoort is a modern seaside town, grown on the back of vast beaches and a motor-racing circuit among the dunes. A sprawling, charmless wasteland of small hotels and wooden weekend cottages, it looks more Belgian than Dutch, but at least I found a hotel without difficulty, with lock-up garaging which may or may not have been necessary. Did the young in Holland enjoy vandalizing cars? I didn't know. Come to think of it, there was very little that I did know about the place. Why so little when it's just across the way? Tulips, bicycles, lots of water, the bridge at Arnhem. Oh yes, and a rather well known red light district in Amsterdam. It didn't seem to add up to much.

I ate an unexpectedly good dinner and stared out of the window at the gathering dark. I wondered briefly if Laurie's hotel was all right and then decided that it was unlikely that the Old Lags would allow themselves to be booked into something that wasn't. And Laurie would know how to get what she wanted better than any of them. All the same, I found it hard to concentrate on what I was eating. I have never been a great believer in coincidence. Some shadowy memory of fey forebears reminds me that in a more or less tenuous way we are all related to each other, and that by extension everything that happens is relative to something else. If that was true, there could be no such thing as coincidence. Just the same, the recent events at Thetfield defeated me. I turned the menu over and scribbled on the back the bare facts as I knew them.

1. Dirk Jager plays golf regularly with a con man.
2. The con man is a convert to fundamentalist Islam.
3. Jager accidentally kills his golf partner.
4. The golf shop at the club is broken into.
5. The club professional disappears.
6. The club professional appears to have died in a car crash at the wheel of a stolen car.

I reviewed the list without enthusiasm. There was an obvious link with 4 and 5 and possibly with 6. But without going into the realms of truly exotic fancy, 1, 2 and 3 defeated me. I sighed and tore the menu up, then immediately felt guilty about it and put the pieces in my pocket instead. The waiter was hovering and on impulse I asked him if he knew of Mijnheer Dirk Jager.

'His name only. He is coming to Zandvoort often, I think. For golf perhaps. There are several clubs near here.'

'He's well known, then?'

The waiter looked dubious. Difficult to tell if he didn't know or whether he thought the question was in bad taste. Laurie had told me that the Dutch disliked obvious signs of wealth, so for all I knew fame was equally undesirable. Too late to put the question another way. Obviously, to be a policeman in someone else's country was even more fraught than in one's own.

The waiter finally said, 'He is very rich,' in a voice that held distinct lack of warmth and went away to look after another table. Oh well, win some, lose some. I went out and walked round for half an hour. It was early in the season and what visitors there were seemed to have taken themselves off in orderly fashion to restaurants or the Casino, so I gave it up and went back to my room and phoned the hotel where Laurie was staying. I hadn't expected her to be in but she was.

'Jager is here,' I told her. 'He passed me in his new Ferrari, going like a bat out of hell. My waiter says he's very rich. Didn't seem over-enthusiastic about him, though.'

I heard her laugh the other end. 'I'm not all that surprised.'

'Why not?'

'I rang Seltje Brinmaker—we're having dinner together later on.'

I said, 'Has she heard of Jager?'

'She said everybody had heard of Jager.' Laurie's voice sounded amused.

'How so?'

'It seems his father was a leading member of the Dutch Nazi party during the Occupation, who saw himself as Holland's post-war President and didn't care who knew it. The day the German troops cleared out in 1945 the Resistance people caught him trying to escape, disguised as a priest. They hanged him from a lamp post in Dam Square.'

Dirk Jager's club was Groenplaats, about twenty minutes' drive out of the town, and I got there about nine-thirty the following morning. There was no Ferrari to be seen in the car park, which indicated that at least I wasn't late and I just hoped I wasn't a lot too early, there being little joy in hanging about someone else's club hoping for that someone to turn up. I locked the Maserati and walked over to the office marked *Secretaris*, hoping that it was true what they said about Dutchmen and that they all spoke English.

The Secretary certainly did. He studied the open letter of introduction from my own club at Harlington, bade me welcome and relieved me of my green fee, which so far as I could work out in my head, cost the Division about thirty pounds. In answer to my question he said that yes, Mr Jager was expected. He would let him know that Mijnheer Angus Straun looked forward to meeting him, and had I heard that there were to be two Dutch entrants for the English Open?

He was an amiable chap, and after a while I got away and had a look around. Holland may or may not have invented the game of golf but today it's still a distinctly up-market sport, awaiting its democratic explosion. Perhaps land is too valuable, or the weather too bad. Either way it adds up to no more than a couple of dozen courses in the whole country, and I knew Groenplaats to be generally recognized as one of the best of the bunch—expensive, exclusive and very well managed, it had often been the setting for some of the country's top competitions. And it looked the part. The clubhouse was a long, single-storeyed building by some architect who knew his job, the front faced with flowerbeds like something out of a bulb grower's catalogue. I'd naturally enough expected the course itself to be flat, but that part of the country isn't short of dunes, and from the clubhouse I was facing a classic links course with narrow fairways and greens hidden between massive bunkers and even more formidable hills of sand. What greens and fairways I could see looked superbly tended, loving care that wasn't over the top in the American fashion but simply making a links that would rate with the best.

I fetched my clubs, changed my shoes in the rather classy locker-room, and moved to the putting green and began to tap a few balls about. Apart from the greenkeeping staff, there appeared to be few members about. Odd for a Saturday. But then one never knew in somebody else's country, maybe it was smarter to play in the afternoon. From the car park I picked up the note of what was something undoubtedly more powerful than an ordinary car. The

Ferrari? I went on tapping balls in. Like everyone else, I putt far better in practice than I do for real and they were beginning to drop from quite phenomenal distances. After a while I was conscious that someone was standing behind me.

'Mr Straun?'

I stopped and looked round. He was watching me with his hands in his pockets, as compact and purposeful as he'd seemed that day at Thetfield. He was bareheaded and a scar across his forehead stood out more than I'd remembered it, probably something to do with the chill of the morning air. He was wearing a cashmere cardigan over a white Lacoste shirt, dark blue canvas slacks above white shoes. There was a large Ping bag at his side and he looked as though he could buy the club, quietly and efficiently, any time he felt like it. The confidence with which his blue, rather prominent eyes were regarding me suggested that he was fully prepared to buy me, too.

I said, 'Jager. Nice to see you again.'

The 'again' didn't throw him. Either he'd recognized me immediately or he'd taken his time observing while I'd been putting. He kicked a loose ball back to me with a flick of his toe. 'Are you here for the golf or to see me?'

'I suppose one could say a little of each.'

Jager rubbed his chin with the back of his hand, an uncharacteristic, nervy gesture. 'I remember you at Thetfield. This is a coincidence?'

'No.' Gareth Evans would be having a fit if he could hear this, I thought, but at least it speeded things up.

'I thought not.' Jager nodded. He looked as though he'd have been disappointed if the answer had been anything else. Those cold eyes of his shifted to mine. 'Shall we have a few holes then, since we're both here? We can talk on the way round if you wish.'

'I'd enjoy that.'

He nodded, as though I'd confirmed what he'd known all the time. 'I play off four. How about you?'

'Six.'

'We'll take a caddy car if you have no objections. It's a long course and I don't imagine you're here for the exercise.' Idiomatically, Jager's English was flawless, only the occasional nasal vowel gave him away. If the Dutch could manage such good English, why couldn't we make some kind of showing at Dutch? Alas, the answer was too easy. Because we didn't have to.

'That's fine,' I said. 'I'm all for a caddy car.' Not strictly true but who was I to go against local custom?

'Is better,' Jager agreed. He went off and collected one from wherever they were kept and we got under way. A watery sun came out from behind a cloud and the grey North Sea turned a kind of slate blue. We were lucky. By Dutch standards we were in for a fine day.

The first hole was a dog-leg to the right, needing a drive of about two hundred yards to the turn and any idea of short cuts discouraged by a line of full grown willows. We made well-nigh identical drives into just about the right place, and watching Jager's swing made me think that I was going to need my two strokes by the end of the day. He wasn't a tall man but his shoulders were enormously broad and he got the ball away with a kind of controlled ferocity. A disciplined swing, too, well groomed by a lot of lessons from someone who knew his job and not one that was likely to break down when the going got rough.

We got in our toy car and whirred busily after the balls. Jager said, 'I remember now that Angela said you'd played a lot of golf at one time.'

'Yes,' I said. 'More than I do now.'

'She's a fine woman. She tells me you are still friends.' He looked at me as though he expected an answer.

'Yes,' I said. 'I suppose so. We see each other sometimes

because of Sam. If it wasn't for him I don't suppose we'd meet.'

'Oh, ja. I was forgetting the boy.'

We got out and played our second shots. It wasn't much more than a hundred and fifty yards to the green and we both made it without difficulty. Jager got in the car and drove it while I walked beside him because it didn't seem worth the trouble of sitting down. He said, 'You are a member of Thetfield?'

He must have known damn well that I wasn't; what he was asking was if I'd been there by chance the day he'd knocked Hunter on the head. 'No,' I told him, 'my club's Harlington, but I've got a temporary job in London at the moment. Thetfield's convenient.'

'Ah.' He nodded as though that had been something he'd known all the time. 'So, about that unfortunate business with poor Hunter. You were not there as policeman, I take it?'

We were at the green. We both played rather good chips and one putted for our pars. We were playing for a ball a hole and I decided that with luck I might not have to buy too many after all, which was probably just as well as I suspected they cost a packet in these parts. I said, 'No, I was not at Thetfield officially.'

He nodded, as though he'd known that, too. 'Well now, Inspector Straun, what about today?' He poked his putter back into that big Ping bag. 'Unofficial, too?'

I looked into those slightly disturbing eyes of his and wondered what my masters would have told me to say. A pointless speculation, seeing that they hadn't taken our mutual interest in Angela into account. Finally I said, 'Yes.'

Jager led the way to the second tee. Short, a hundred and sixty yards or so down to a little island entirely surrounded by bunkers, a kind of target in the sand. He said, 'I left my address. When your people want me for the inquest, I'll come. No trouble.' A thought seemed to strike him and he added, 'So your people haven't tied this up with the local police?'

I shook my head. 'No.'

'Man, then you'd better keep it unofficial.' Jager frowned, and his Dutch accent became suddenly more pronounced. 'You people wouldn't be liking it if Dutch police started chasing after someone in England, I think.' Which was much what Gareth Evans had said, I remembered. There was something to be said for cultural excursions after all.

We took a five iron apiece and we both managed to hit the green. There was getting to be something of a ritual about this business of talking and driving by turns. I put Gareth Evans out of my mind as best I could. I said, 'Look, Jager, I'm not here about Hunter. As a matter of fact, I don't even know the date of the inquest.'

For once he didn't make his shot but just stared at me. For a moment I got the impression that, given the chance, he'd have seized me by the throat and wrung the next bit out of me, but although I saw his knuckles go white round the grip of his putter he kept a hold on himself pretty well. Finally he said, 'So what is it that you do want?'

It seemed an opportunity to take a leaf from his book so I made my putt, all of eight feet, which probably justified the time I took over it. I had my doubts about it, but the ball dropped safely enough.

'Good putt.' Jager lined up his own ball without raising his eyes. He hadn't more than four feet to go but he gave the thing his full attention. For a wild moment I thought he'd missed it, because the ball swung round the lip of the cup for a moment before it finally dropped. Halved again, I wasn't complaining but wondered just how long I could keep this up.

'So?' The word sounded wrung out of him.

I said, 'I came to give you a friendly and unofficial word about your friend Mr Wong.'

Well, I'd hoped to get results with that one and I wasn't disappointed, because the word 'Wong' stopped Jager in his tracks and he swung his head sideways at me as though he was trying to get me with his horns. 'So what about my friend Wong?'

The sixth sense sounded out its warning but when you're half way over the edge of Niagara there isn't any way out but on. I drew a deep breath and got it over with. 'Usually,' I said, 'we warn people like Freddy Wong off and the whole thing's kept quiet, but unfortunately he's wangled himself diplomatic immunity and we can't touch him. But it's only fair to tell you that he's known to the police both in England and America as a confidence man. A confidence man—'

'I know what is a confidence man.' Jager pointed due ahead with his putter. 'The third tee is over there, Inspector. And I know all about Freddy Wong.'

'In that case,' I said, 'we may as well concentrate on the game.' In the circumstances, the best I could manage in the way of dignified withdrawal.

Jager let out a great snort of laughter. 'My God, Straun, do you people really think I got to be one of the richest men in Holland without being able to spot a crook when I see one? Do I look that much of a fool?'

I said, 'Very big people have been taken to the cleaners by con men before now.' I was furious with Gareth Evans and his friend Todhunter and not exactly ecstatic about Angela but I was damned if I was going to wag my tail at their tycoon while he kicked me.

Jager said affably, 'Well, I haven't. My dear chap, I assure you I have no illusions about Freddy Wong. I wouldn't buy a postage stamp off him, but he amuses me and he plays a very sound game of golf. And so do you, come to that.'

'Thank you.'

'But I don't understand why the London police should waste time and money sending one of their officers over here to warn a Dutchman that he is about to—' he paused only briefly—'to have his pocket picked.'

I said, 'Perhaps it depends which Dutchman it is.'

He nodded, pleased. 'As you say. Now we've finished business, we can get on with the game.' He glanced at me in query. 'That pleases you?'

'Of course.' I was pleased too, because he'd liked the flattery enough to overlook the possibility that Angela might have started the whole thing going in the first place. Dirk Jager was bright, I told myself, but not that bright.

'Good. Still your honour, I think.'

I enjoyed the game. The course was a good one and in spite of a two stroke handicap difference we were pretty evenly matched. Outside of the big tournaments there's not a lot to be got out of the blow by blow description of a round of golf—at each hole someone does this or that and unless you've got a lot of money on it the only thing that matters is if someone does a hole in one or actually drops down dead. On this particular Saturday morning at Groenplaats neither happened, but the game ended oddly for all that. By the sixteenth I'd succeeded, by some inspired fluking, to get a hole ahead, and I could sense Jager's irritation. God knows why it riled him. Perhaps by his standards he wasn't playing as well as usual, perhaps he was just a bad loser but, either way, he didn't like it and it was beginning to show.

Our drives from the seventeenth tee were much alike, mine the shorter by a couple of yards. The lie was good enough, and I hit a decent six iron to the edge of the green, then waited to see what Jager would do. I've no idea what club he chose but, whatever it was, it didn't suit the moment because he hooked his shot just enough to land the ball in the short rough and with fifty yards still to go.

'Hard luck,' I said.

I said it and meant it, because with the kind of golf Jager had been playing there has to be an element of luck when something goes that wrong. I heard him mutter something to himself in Dutch but that was all, and we walked over together to assess the damage. As it happened, it could have been a lot worse, because the ball was sitting up pretty well, three or four feet from a willow tree.

'No problem,' I told him. Unnecessarily, because the man could see for himself.

'Ja. Could be worse.' He collected a nine iron from his bag, had a look round and addressed the ball. For a player of his standard it was an easy enough shot, a brief fifty yards with just one bunker at an angle, midway between ourselves and the green. There were no branches to get in the way, and with the ball almost teed up on its tuft of coarse sea grass it needed only a gentle flick to plonk it down somewhere within a few feet of the hole. Jager drew his wrists back in a stroke that was rather less than a half swing and in some way managed to just catch his descending club head on the trunk of the tree. It was only a glancing blow, insufficient to stop the stroke completely but enough to break the rhythm and set it off course, and with a distinct *thunk* the broad blade of the club bit into the ground at least an inch further back than he must have intended, chewing up a massive divot and projecting the ball forward at about half its intended velocity. There was a momentary blur of white and then a soft thud as the ball dropped soggily into the sand of the bunker.

This time I didn't say 'bad luck' because I'd said it once already and felt that perhaps silent sympathy was best. For a moment Jager didn't say anything. He just stood there, staring after the ball as though he didn't believe what had happened and I watched his face go bright red, then deathly pale. Then abruptly he turned towards the tree. Like most willows, its branches grew quite low down and there was

one about five feet from the ground, a gnarled, bent affair
with a hole in it where I suppose it had been struck by some
kind of rot. With a completely expressionless face Jager
lifted his nine iron and inserted its head in the hole, then
with a sudden bunching of his powerful shoulders be began
to wind the steel shaft of the club around the branch.

I just stood there and watched him. I don't really know
what surprised me more—the sheer cold-blooded destruc-
tiveness of the thing or the feat of strength involved. A
modern golf club is constructed of tempered steel, designed
to withstand years of sharp concussion as well as general
knock-around abuse. I had heard of strong men bending
pokers in their bare hands, but pokers are made of iron. I
know I found myself wondering in an academic kind of way
just how far the damn thing would go—how far Jager could
make it go. In fact, he almost got it wound into a complete
shining chrome hoop before it snapped at the head with a
crack like a rifle shot.

For a few moments Jager stood with his back to me and
I think I heard him give a kind of sigh. Then he tossed away
what was left of the club and turned round to face me. He
was smiling and there was an odd look in his eyes that made
me feel uncomfortable, but that was all. In his place I should
have been acutely embarrassed, but Jager seemed to have
accepted the incident as the most natural thing in the world.

'Your hole, my dear Straun,' he said. 'And your match.
Now let's go to the club house and I'll buy you lunch.'

CHAPTER 8

It was a good lunch, better than I'd expected, immaculately
served in an oak-panelled dining-room overlooking the
eighteenth green. The place was half full, and I put the

membership down as being a bit older than our own equivalent but well dressed and full of get-up-and-go. We ate a sort of prawn remoulade, filet of pork sautéd in cream and brandy and some first-class cheese drawn from a selection you wouldn't believe. It made memories of pork pie and chips back at Harlington something to wince over, although Jager obviously classed it as pretty ordinary pub fare and washed it down with Perrier water throughout, which seemed like a good idea, with driving still to be done.

Perhaps he read my thoughts because he said gloomily, 'One has to watch the traffic police.' I think he must quite genuinely have forgotten because he added, 'Of course, you *are* the police. But that wouldn't do you much good with our sons of bitches. They'd book their own fathers if they knew who they were.'

All the world hates a traffic cop, but I was surprised that he'd be so meticulous over the drink-drive laws while quite obviously disregarding speed restrictions, a distinction for which I had a certain sympathy.

I said, 'I heard somewhere that you like Ferraris. It can't be easy to keep those down to 100 k.p.h.'

Jager's mouth twisted into what I suppose passed as a smile. 'Speeding tickets can be fixed—a drink charge can't.'

Well, you can't say fairer than that. 'Then I suppose it was you who passed me coming up here yesterday—someone went by me in a red Mondial like a ton of bricks.'

He nodded. 'I tell you, man, that's the trouble: you stick out like a—' He looked down at his hand. 'How do you say it? A hurt thumb?'

'Sore thumb.' He wasn't often caught out.

'Ja—sore thumb.' Jager caught the eye of the steward, who promptly broke off from what he was doing and brought us coffee instead. When it was poured and the man had gone away he went on with a kind of Nordic gloom, 'I like to drive fast, which is more than I can say of most of my countrymen. The only good car I saw yesterday was a Maserati and that was so properly in the slow lane.'

I said, 'I always go so properly in countries where I don't speak the language.'

Jager stared at me. 'You?'

'Yes,' I confessed. 'I'm afraid so.' Cars, the great leveller. A left-over passion from schooldays, but there was more point to it than gambling and it did no more harm to the environment than blasting birds or chasing foxes. Less, really.

Jager rubbed his chin again—I couldn't be sure whether it signified that he was amused or simply puzzled. 'I must say, man,' he said, 'it's an odd car for a policeman to drive.'

'They drive Porsche 911s over here.'

He gave me that rather sinister grin of his. 'That's true. But they don't own them.' He paused and remembered something. 'Angela says you write books.'

What he meant was that he'd finally worked out where the money came from, which would have been rather bad form for most people but an understandable quirk in a millionaire.

I said yes, I'd written a few.

He nodded, apparently satisfied, and I thought what an extraordinary character he was with his ability to switch from that cold, murderous rage to this apparently genuine affability, sparked by no more than the fact that we had in common a liking for fast cars. It could have been two different men. He stood up abruptly. 'We look at your car. Where did you leave it?'

'In the car park.' Where did he think I'd left the thing?

Jager frowned. 'I didn't see it.'

'Well, that's where I left it.' There was something slightly paranoid about the man's change of moods, the jump of suspicion into those cold blue eyes. Jager scribbled a signature on the bill the steward was holding and clumped his way out of the club, virtually ignoring the odd fellow member who greeted him in passing. It was easy enough to spot his Ferrari, parked against the wall of what was probably a mower shed. It was a bright red wedge of a car that looked almost ludicrously exotic alongside a herd of dark-coloured family saloons.

Jager said shortly, 'There's mine.' He didn't say, 'Where's yours?' and I got the drift all right.

'You can't see mine from here,' I said. 'It's up the other end.' It was clear enough why he hadn't spotted the Maserati, the car park was shaped like a horseshoe with the mower shed in the middle. All the same, I didn't feel him relax until my car was in front of him and he could see for himself that I hadn't been having him on.

'Ja.' He recognized it and was satisfied. 'This one I saw.' He prowled round my toy for a while, then said abruptly, 'I'm not good on Maserati models. What's this one?'

'They call this the Khamsin,' I told him. 'It's a wind. They name all Maserati models after winds—Mistral, Khamsin, Ghibli and so on.' I opened it up and we looked at the engine, something of a lump compared to a Ferrari but with a lot of brute strength about it. The Khamsin's engine bay is fairly cramped with engraved cam covers and complex plumbing and my audience was impressed all right. He asked a lot of sensible questions and then we went back to his own vehicle and we did the whole thing over again for my benefit with the Ferrari.

'Sit in it!' Jager said. 'Sit in it!'

I sat in it and yes, it felt pretty good. Is there a man with soul so dead that the sight of a wood-rimmed steering-wheel with a prancing horse decorating the middle doesn't do something to him deep down?

'*Une orgasme véritable*,' a car-mad friend had once so described his own to me, and I saw his point. I looked over the rest of the offering, the famous Ferrari open gate for the gear shift, the rampant horse in the middle of the steering-wheel. From under the dashboard I glimpsed something blue. Blue. I inspected the tape-deck closely and with admiration so as to get a better look, but I'd been right first time. The same London Route Guide that I used myself. Bully for Angela, ten out of ten for observation.

'What you think, man? Pretty good finish, eh?'

Dirk Jager was peering through the window, doing his celebrated impersonation of a kid with a new toy. I'd no idea who his favourite car salesman was but he must have been a very happy man.

'Yes,' I said, 'great.' And I meant it. I got out reluctantly. It wasn't the car I minded leaving so much as that book, but I could hardly look up the annotated maps under the man's very nose. But I'd have given a lot to see them.

'You have driven a Mondial?'

'No,' I said. 'A Dino once, that's all.'

'The Dino's a boy's car,' Jager said. 'But then, I've never driven a Khamsin, come to that.' He looked at me with what seemed more interest than he'd shown to date. 'Look, man, I have an idea. You say you're spending the night in Amsterdam?'

'Yes,' I said, 'that was the idea.'

'I tell you, that's good. I have something Angela asked for. You could take it back to her, right?' There was something slightly unreal about the all good pals bit, but I nodded. The man had bought me lunch, after all, and it didn't seem much to ask. Just so long as—

'*Trek je er niets van aan!*' Jager let out one of his short barks of laughter and shook his head. 'My dear fellow, there is no need to worry. I promise not to turn you into a drug courier.' He seemed to have an uncanny knack of knowing what was going on in someone else's mind.

I said, 'I'm glad to help,' but I was wondering how I

could talk myself into getting back into his car without having him breathing down my neck. After all, I could hardly stand here in the middle of Holland and ask if I might borrow his road map of London without arousing some small *frisson* of suspicion. I had what seemed like a good idea. 'Look,' I said, 'if we're going to Amsterdam and you'd like to try a Maserati, why don't we drive each other's cars?'

He thought it over. It didn't take him long, and those curious eyes of his bored into mine and for a moment I thought he was going to refuse, but he didn't. Instead he banged me on the shoulder and made noises like being pleased.

'By God, man, a good idea!'

I said, 'Only just take it easy, will you. You may be able to buy your way out of speed traps, but I can't.'

Jager nodded briefly, and I sensed he was ready to go at this very moment, like a small boy who wants to ride his birthday bicycle. It was an odd reaction from a man who was rich enough to indulge himself in almost anything, but then rich men tend to be odd. He said, 'I want to make a phone call. Anything you want out of your car?'

'I'll make one too, if I may.' It wasn't difficult to pick up this and that from the Maserati, the this discreetly covering the that, which was my own copy of the London map.

The clubhouse wasn't short of telephones, and one could imagine a fair proportion of members breaking off before a game to have a quick five minutes with their stockbroker. I ensconced myself within a plastic bubble and rang the Victoria Hotel where Laurie was staying, on the off-chance that she might be there, which she wasn't, so I tried Seltje Brinmaker instead. Did Dutch literary agents work Saturday afternoons? Or have an answering service? For all I knew she could have her office in her apartment—I mulled over the permutation of this and that while the ringing tone purred a few times. I never did think to ask which one was right but the girl answered.

'*U spreekt met Brinmaker.*'

'Angus Straun,' I said. 'I'm sorry to trouble you, but is Laurie there?'

'Oh hi!' The maddening unconscious bi- and tri-lingual switch that the Dutch and Swiss seem to manage better than anyone. 'No, she's not, but I'm off to take her shopping at the Bijenkorf, as a matter of fact. Any message?'

'Tell her I'll be back at the hotel at—' When, for God's sake? 'I'm at the golf club near Zandvoort,' I said. 'How long by road?'

'On your own?'

'I'll have a guide.'

'Great. I'll tell her you'll be there at eight.'

Just listening to her filled me with confidence. She sounded a lovely lady and I asked her to join us for dinner but she laughed and said it wasn't on, but maybe tomorrow.

'Ready, Straun?' Jager getting impatient behind me, he really was like a small boy.

'Is that the man himself in the background?' Seltje was saying in my ear.

'Yes.'

'Well, watch it.'

I thanked her genuinely and put the phone down. I had a feeling that Dirk Jager was not a man who liked to be kept waiting.

Getting from Zandvoort to Amsterdam is easy enough when you know how, which is to take the ring road round nearby Haarlem and then head east on the big, six-lane ribbon of the A5. There was plenty of traffic but it's easy to follow one's own car, particularly if it happens to be bright red, and Jager was taking it easy. Which was just as well, as we weren't something you could overlook. We hadn't travelled more than half a dozen kilometres before a *Politie* Porsche had tucked itself in behind me and stayed there. It must have been obvious that I knew of his arrival and that I wasn't going to do anything silly, so I suppose he just wanted to have a look.

It was a pleasant thirty miles or so while I got the hang of the Ferrari, which was a skittish and high-bred creature after the rather brutish muscle power of the Khamsin. By the time we reached the outskirts of Amsterdam I'd have been prepared to let the beast have its head but, although the police car turned off, the traffic became solid and I was thankful to have to do no more than follow my own familiar number plate in front of me.

Amsterdam's parking problem is horrendous was the way my guide book had summed up the situation and I felt no need to quarrel with that. Where *did* one park? I wondered. The odd sideways glance showed either unbroken lines of cars or stacked bicycles and my sole previous visit to the city had left no true impression as to how narrow the streets were. It was getting dark and the entire city appeared to be on the move, flowing over the canal bridges like demented lemmings, walkers and cyclists milling in and out the cars as though they were glued to the ground. I was glad it wasn't my problem and crawled blindly behind my guide, hoping that the Ferrari wasn't going to overheat, which it didn't. We skirted an open space I vaguely remembered as Dam Square, swung suddenly sideways in front of a vast store and were without warning swallowed up in the entrance maw of a car park. Well, bully for Jager, I thought. But then, after all, it was his town.

I exchanged my road book for his, slipping the latter into my coat pocket and wondered how long it would be before he noticed the difference. Almost certainly not until he wanted to refer to his circled properties again and, with any luck, by then he'd be pushed to even guess what had happened. Even if he connected the incident with me the chances were that he'd put the switch down to a genuine mistake. Or so I hoped, as I climbed out and we exchanged keys and complimented each other on our respective cars.

'Now we can go to my office,' Jager said. 'It is quickest through the Kerkstraat. You know Amsterdam?'

'No,' I said. I wondered if I'd have been safer to have said yes but there are times when one is doomed to lose either way and this looked like being one of them.

'Good. We shall have one drink on the way. The place will amuse you.'

I wasn't mad keen on the idea. In some ill-defined but nigglingly insistent way I felt happier with Dirk Jager as the glacial tycoon, not going along with this all boys together bit. I wondered what he was like with women. Presumably he had to have something acceptable or Angela would never have put up with him, although there was always money.

'Just one, then,' I agreed. There was still forty-five minutes before I was due to meet Laurie.

Jager nodded as though the answer amused him. 'You meeting your friend, eh? I'll show you lots of friends.'

He didn't wait for an answer. He just led the way out of the park and into the crowded grey streets, splashed here and there with the light reflected from the shop windows, and I went with him as he turned east from the Damrak and dived into the warren beyond. In its own way, walking through Amsterdam requires almost as much attention as driving, because bicycles creep silently up on you from all sides and if you keep your peripheral vision for them you're liable to miss the sandy excavations the local services dig at regular intervals as they shore up the city's precarious wooden underpinning.

Kerkstraat. We crossed the bridge over a narrow canal and suddenly there was the feeling of being in a different lifestyle. *Church Street*, which was just about as far as one could go with inappropriate names. My single previous visit to Amsterdam had been no more than a time-killing exercise between trains, and it had not included a visit to the city's raunchier parts, but a quick glance in the shop windows and the purposeful look on the faces of the sightseers as they digested the multi-lingual neon signs made it clear enough where we were.

Jager towed me into a waterside equivalent of the Avenue Clichy and I wondered if perhaps I'd found what it was that made him tick. Amsterdam's red light district is the kind of paradox that fascinates sociologists and delights the chaps at the tills, but all in all not that surprising. Just as we are exhorted to understand that New York is not America, Amsterdam is not altogether representative of the Netherlands; nevertheless a kind of pre-war Port Said on the Amstel seems curiously out of place under grey skies and the steady, fine rain.

'Good for tourism,' Jager was saying.

Well, yes. I watched a squad of blue-rinsed American grandmothers approach, shepherded by a courier who seemed to be taking his job as seriously as though he was escorting them to a Bible class. I rather expected his flock to march down the street looking neither to left nor right, ignoring the suspender-belted girls sitting pretty in their shop-fronted bedrooms. Wrong again. They not only studied the offerings with approval but showed a lively interest in the porn shows as well. One sprightly old soul clutching her mink about her tottered to the nearest centre of culture and stared entranced at a large blow-up of someone dressed as a gorilla taking a considerable liberty with a large-busted lady in a terai hat and nothing else.

'For Chrissake, girls, come look at this!' You could hear her from the other side of the street. The girls flocked to her and cried, 'Hell, it's not like Little Rock!' Well no, it was not like Little Rock. It was not like Little Rock at all.

'Most popular sight in Amsterdam,' Jager was saying. He took me by the arm and pushed me through a doorway into a kind of pink gloom. A bar, three half-circles of upholstered seats, an empty, spotlit stage. A rather villainous-looking Indonesian in a dinner jacket materialized behind the bar. The drinks list on the wall behind him named the place as 'Shangri-La'.

'*Goedenavond, Mijneer.*' The greeting was not for me.

''*avond, Nim.*' Jager gave him a nod, rather as though we were in the Garrick. To me he asked, 'What are you drinking?'

I studied the empty stage without enthusiasm. My old station sergeant used to say, 'I'm all for a little good clean vice,' and I suppose honest whoredom is a state hallowed at least by time, but I share the average copper's distrust of the associated porn scene. Maybe it's true that if you enjoy watching people doing in public what normally goes on in private there's no great harm done, but there's always the point where someone demands that much extra in the way of stimulation, which is where drugs come in.

And drugs mean organized crime.

I considered Jager's offer of a drink and kicked myself mentally for getting myself into my present situation. At the inquisitive age of nineteen I'd attended one '*petit spectacle*' in a cellar off the Place Pigalle and had no great desire to see another. On the other hand, there's a knack to declining any form of hospitality. A girl could have extricated herself easily enough by saying simply, 'No, thanks, darling—not my scene.' But different for chaps. Any form of refusal I made to Jager was going to say, in effect: 'Indulge your perverted fancies if you must, but don't include me in that kind of thing,' which was too clinically British to be considered.

'*Twee whisky.*' Jager had evidently got tired of waiting for me to make up my mind and the barman reached for the bottle. Behind him the curtain stirred and two more young men slipped into the room. They were white, unpleasant-looking, dressed in regulation leather jackets and jeans and I felt a prickle of disquiet. Why so? After all, the red light district wasn't a place where you expect to find the nicest people. I glanced at Jager but he was sipping his drink and watching the stage, upon which a couple had appeared somewhat inappropriately dressed in tiger skins.

Abruptly, the lights went out.

For a fleeting instant I thought that this was simply the dimming of the house lights prior to the start of the show, but there was no stage lighting either, and besides, I had my personal alarm bells ringing loud and clear by this time, signalling that I'd been a bloody fool to come into this particular den in the first place and that now it would be a good thing if I left it as quickly as possible. Somebody grabbed me by the arm and I threw a punch in the general direction of where the grabber might be. My first dug satisfactorily into something human, there was a grunt and the hand fell away.

'Straun!' It was Jager's voice calling urgently but my warning system said no, and this time I paid attention. There had been perhaps ten feet between the bar and the back row of chairs, so I took three quick strides straight ahead and stood still. Behind me there was a lot of grunting and scuffling going on but I paid little attention to it, my mind being lost in the past. I don't know how many years ago, but I'd once helped raid a cabaret in Soho for the desperate crime of flogging drink after hours. At the time we'd thought that we'd got all the exits effectively sealed but had subsequently lost the lot when the management had nipped rather smartly backstage and then—by way of the dressing-rooms—to the fire escape.

'Straun—' But he didn't sound to me like a man who was being beaten up, and anyway, I thought unsympathetically, he'd chosen the place. I reached for the back row of chairs, found one of them and climbed over it. Already my eyes were getting used to things and the world I was in was becoming rather less pitch black. I got across two more chairs and my feet hit the hard surface of the stage at the same moment that I spotted a chink of light. A door? I made a dive for it and trod on a bare foot. Judging by the squeal that followed almost in my ear it must have been the lady in the tiger skin but I didn't stop to find out.

'Sorry!' I said. Why does one say these nonsenses? I reached the door, kicked it open and dived through to find myself in a tiny alcove with an unshaded light-bulb illuminating a mirror on a table, a chair and bits of this and that hung up on string. There was another open door and I went through it like a scalded cat, only to find myself in some kind of yard full of rubbish bins and bicycles. But there was another door, praise God, and I yanked it open and almost fell into the garish street beyond.

Christ! I glanced round to get my bearing and discovered that the rosy glow surrounding me was a neon sign. I looked up at it.

SHANGRI-LA
Live Sex on Stage

Same building, different door, a bit further down the road. It struck me forcibly that I'd do best to get as far away from the place as possible in case the people inside came after me, but as I stood working this out there was a lot of flashing blue lights and three police cars came up, spilling their occupants at the double. They were probably heading for the building at my back, but so far as I was concerned they were heading straight for me.

'Don't just *stand* there!' It was Laurie at my side, her arm through mine, and I fell into step obediently. Someone had the other arm—I had a quick glance and found it was a dark-haired plump lass I'd never set eyes on before. Seltje Brinmaker? Two policemen were running purposefully straight at me and I jumped as Laurie suddenly let out a squeal of laughter and a gabble of incomprehensible Dutch, at which her friend leaned across me and hooted something back. I never did ask what it was but it must have been something fairly ribald because the cop paused long enough to grin at the two of them before pounding past. I heard their boots on the tiled entrance of the Shangri-La and a crowd began to converge to see what was going on.

'I think we should get out of here,' Seltje said.

Nobody disagreed with her.

CHAPTER 9

I wasn't at my best on the journey back, which was understandable because it had been a long way to go to warn someone of what he knew already. Also I was uncomfortably aware that the Amsterdam episode was straight low comedy. A bloody marvel, really, I said, that at the time of my ignominious rescue I hadn't managed to lose my trousers.

'A pity,' Laurie said. 'Seltje laughed enough as it was. If your pants had been round your ankles, it would have made her day.' We were in the ferry bar, drinking duty-free whisky at about the same price as it was at home. She patted my hand. 'Relax, darling. Joke.' Her smile was wifely. Perhaps not too wifely, and I wondered why Angela's ghost took so long to be laid.

'All right,' I said, 'I know it was funny.' But I was not particularly amused, having allowed myself to be led into a potentially unpleasant situation without even a bleat of protest. I didn't know for sure what was supposed to have happened to me at the Shangri-La, presumably I was due to end up being photographed on stage in what used to be called 'compromising circumstances'. The tabloids would certainly have loved it.

RANDY POLICEMAN RUNS RIOT
CID Man's Wicked Weekend Away

But to what end? Why me? I didn't know but I was grateful to the girls all the same and said so, adding, 'It was the one bit of luck of the day.'

'Luck?' Laurie gave the idea her attention as though she hadn't thought of it that way before. 'Well, I suppose it was luck that Seltje and I had been having tea in the Bijenkorf just as you two were driving in. Two bright red Italian nonsenses—we could hardly miss you. You practically stopped the traffic.'

I said, 'But of course it was luck you just happened to follow us.'

'You must be joking,' Laurie said. 'Seltje and I could see the way you were heading. We thought if you went into one of those shows it would be fun to hang about and just happen to bump into you as you came out.'

'Good for the girlish giggle.'

'Well—yes.' She smiled faintly. 'Forget it, darling. Seltje won't split. Tell me what you're hugging your London guide for.'

I'd forgotten I'd brought it up from the car. 'It isn't mine, as a matter of fact.' I'd forgotten I'd not told her about it. Or perhaps forgot on purpose, so that I wouldn't have to explain why I'd been visiting Angela. Well, that was just too bad, because she'd have to know now anyway. I told her.

Laurie frowned. 'He's bound to find out.'

'Sooner or later,' I agreed. 'But with any luck, later. And by then almost anyone could have made the switch. It could even have been an accident.'

'You've an optimistic nature, I'll say that for you.' She

flipped the book open at the appropriate page, which wasn't difficult because it was neatly flagged with a piece of folded paper. The close-printed maps of the city didn't show up too well in the bar's dimmish lighting, but it was easy enough to see that Jager had marked six places in all, though fairly roughly. In each case he'd used a red fibre tip pen to make a circle with a diameter of about a centimetre—a neat enough annotation in itself but, on a map of that size, it was hardly pinpoint accuracy.

'Half a centimetre on the map must be the thick end of a hundred yards on the ground,' I complained. 'He could have been marking damn near anything.' Against the bar a group of youths began to raise their voices in obscene argument. I looked up, Laurie shook her head.

'You're off duty. Concentrate.'

Concentration wasn't easy, but I found a notebook and scribbled down the half dozen locations with as near an identification as I could manage.

1. HIGHBURY. Corner of Austin Park and Carter St.
2. HAMPSTEAD. Junction of Overton St and Webley St.
3. FINCHLEY. Corner of Finchley Rd and Leeds Rd.
4. MUSWELL HILL. Corner of Sebastopol St and Sales Row.
5. HIGHGATE CORNER of Park Gate and Queens Rd.
6. GOLDERS GREEN. Junction of Compton Crescent and Basildon St.

I tossed the finished effort over to Laurie. 'That's as near as I can make it. Any suggestions?'

'It's impossible to say without having a look.' She nibbled the end of her pencil. 'I mean, there may be some kind of obvious link—like each one pinpointing a pub or a garage or something. Obviously they've all got something in common.'

'Yes,' I said, 'they're in London.'

'We can do better than that.' She looked at her watch. 'What time do we dock?'

I looked through the porthole at the rain lashing down on to the grey North Sea. It didn't look very welcoming. I hazarded a guess. 'About midday.'

It hadn't been the sort of weekend that was going to end with me getting a time of arrival right and it was past four when we finally reached Kinnerton Street. I got the cases out of the car and Laurie went round the flat doing whatever it is women find so important to do when they've been away for even the shortest of times. There was a pile of mail for her but she didn't open it, the natural perversity of characters other than one's own.

I asked her if she wanted a cup of coffee.

'Yes, all right.' She was frowning with concentration, putting a dress away. 'Angus, are you going to tell your people that Jager sent those etchings round to our hotel before we left?'

Well, was I? 'No,' I said, 'I don't think so.' They'd been left at the reception desk with a note: *Sorry about the trouble last night. D.J.* I found the filter papers and stuck one in the machine. 'It doesn't really have much bearing.'

'At least it proves he really did have something in his office he wanted you to pass on to Angela.'

I said, 'Or it proves he went out later and bought something Angela *might* have wanted.'

'I may be thick,' Laurie said, 'but that doesn't make sense. Jager told you he had something Angela had asked him for. Well, it seems she asked him for a couple of etchings, because that's what she's got. Damn it, Angus, you looked.'

'I know,' I agreed, 'it's just that I happen to know that Angela loathes etchings—hates anything black and white on the wall, as a matter of fact. She'd never have asked for those things in a hundred years.'

'So why did Jager give them to her?'

'I imagine he wanted some reason for inviting me to his office and a present for Angela was as good a reason as any.'

I thought that one over and it seemed to make sense. I went on, 'Etchings were probably the first thing that came to mind. I mean—they're on sale everywhere over there. If you can't afford a diamond from Amsterdam, try an etching instead.'

'I suppose you've checked all this out with Angela?' The deceptive casual bit, which I should have seen a mile away but didn't.

Instead I said, 'You know damn well I haven't phoned anyone since we got back.'

'You could have phoned her from the boat, for all I know.' Ridiculous, and unlike Laurie, who might explode but was not petty. Still, it had been that kind of weekend and I didn't altogether blame her.

Nevertheless, this resentment of Angela was something new. Up till now the two had seemed to get on pretty well together, but then, up till now my ex-wife had simply been Sam's mother. Certainly I hadn't previously been running round golf courses on her behalf.

'The only person I've rung since we got back is Gareth Evans.' I suppose my voice sounded defensive. 'It seems I have to report direct to Todhunter tomorrow, which is something I could do without.'

Laurie said nothing.

'Look,' I told her, 'you've got a mass of mail to go through. I'd better leave you to it.' My own borrowed one-room desirable apartment in Hallam Mews did not exactly call, but perhaps it was diplomatic in the circumstances.

'It would probably be better,' Laurie agreed. 'You'll be wanting to report to Angela, anyway.'

I thought briefly and charitably of the late Dr Crippen but kept my mouth shut, to be rewarded with the gift of memory. 'It's the first Monday of the quarter,' I reminded her. 'The Bowyers Society. I missed the last one.'

Laurie gave me a look full of disenchantment. 'If you're

taking an evening off from the law I'd have thought you might write a few lines. You've a book due for delivery in two months and you'll be pushed enough as it is without jolly get-togethers of mediæval warfare fanatics.'

'Research,' I told her. 'Research.'

And so it was, in a way. Nobody writes seriously about the past without having at least an enthusiasm for his period and I'd written my first novel on the Hundred Years War for fun, nobody being more surprised than myself when it had made me a lot of money. With three books behind me I could, in theory, support myself by writing full time. But I liked being a policeman and I enjoyed the slightly schizophrenic world in which I could be one thing during the day and something entirely different at night. Such as the company of the Bowyers Society, which met at the Walker Gallery four times a year to discuss the finer points of the archer's craft with an erudition that would probably have amazed the men who actually fought at Agincourt. A pretty esoteric lot, but I always tried to attend the Bowyers' meetings and on this occasion I felt that I deserved it.

''Evening, Mr Straun. Geoff and me laid on a bit of nosh in the ante-room.'

'Good evening, Mr Walker.' One did not address the elder of the Walker brothers as Sid, because I doubted if even his own mother had ventured that. The Walker brothers looked like something from a steel engraving of a Regency prize fight and sounded like television actors playing the part. Their antecedents were a closed book even to me, and it wasn't for want of trying, but whatever they sounded or looked like, the Walker Gallery in Avery Street had a worldwide reputation as a saleroom for mediæval artefacts. The brothers themselves were no fools either.

I went through into the ante-room, which was the small saleroom tarted up a bit for the occasion. There was absolutely no reason why the Walkers should lend their premises

to a crowd of amiable loonies. The cynical might have
suggested that from time to time a few of us might spend
more than we could reasonably afford at one of the Walkers'
sales, and the Bowyers were simply good for trade, but that
would have been ungrateful. Sid and Geoff could sell just
about anything that came their way ten times over. By their
lights they were a public-spirited pair.

''Evening, Straun! You'd better get yourself some caviar
before your fellow members clear it up.' Grenville Matson
pushed his way through the score or so members who were
milling around the Walkers' idea of a bit of nosh. He was a
huge, red-faced man with shoulders like a bull who looked
as though he might be something in the meat trade but was,
in fact, the Matson of Matson and Partridge, estate agents
and surveyors, who seemed to handle the sales of half the
commercial properties in London.

I said hello and found myself some cold salmon and a
glass of Chablis, but Matson pursued me.

'You remember the querbole I was trying to get hold of
last year?'

A sinking of the heart. The querbole was the hard leather
helmet favoured by the Black Prince's archers, and the one
Matson had run to earth in a castle on the Welsh marches
had been something that had excited him as much as a
multi-million pound property deal. What had possessed me
to tell him that the thing was a fake? I wondered. I'd thought
it was but I certainly hadn't known. Why couldn't I keep
my nose out of other people's bad buys?

'I owe you,' Matson was saying. 'I got Tony Lamont to
have a look at it and he said you were absolutely right. It
was a Florentine copy.'

'Good,' I said. 'I'm glad you weren't done.' I was, too.
Genuinely glad, although I'd never heard of Tony Lamont,
someone who presumably knew a lot more than I did, but
on this occasion my confrère, no less.

'It's not the money,' Matson said, and I believed him. 'One just doesn't enjoy looking a fool. Have lunch with me next week.'

I reminded him that I was a policeman and lunch at a predictable time tended to be a rarity, which was true. Also true that I didn't particularly want his lunch.

'Well, damn it, there must be something—' He was the kind of man who liked to keep his accounts straight, and the fact that I'd done something for him meant that now he had to do something for me and I was being difficult not accepting his lunch. As it happens, I was saved by the chairman tinkling his little bell to remind us that it was time we sat ourselves down and listened to our guest speaker who had something erudite to impart about mediæval arrow flights and the Archer's Paradox.

Mostly I paid attention at the Bowyers' little talks but the mathematics of arrow behaviour was a bit beyond me and I let my attention wander. On this occasion it was only capable of wandering one way, and after a few minutes I gave up trying to follow the effect of vibration on the arrow shaft in flight and my mind went back to Messrs Jager and Wong instead. Was Freddy Wong really cultivating the Dutchman on behalf of his adopted country or was that just Todhunter of the Foreign Office having a flight of fancy? Was there any way Bill Tilling could be linked with the Constantines? If the latter hadn't a cast-iron alibi for their van, there might have been, but even Stephenos couldn't have spirited the damn thing out of the police pound.

I still hadn't got anywhere by the time the talk ended with the usual polite round of applause. It had been a long weekend and I was looking forward to going home and getting some sleep, but I found time to buttonhole Grenville Matson before he left.

'There's something you *could* do for me. If it's not too much trouble—'

'My dear chap, of course!' He thought I was going to have his lunch after all, but he was wrong. Instead I handed him a copy of the circled areas I'd found in Jager's London map book.

I said, 'I drove past these addresses before coming here this evening. They're ordinary commercial properties. Would you have a look and see if they've got anything in common for me?'

Matson took the list. 'How do you mean—in common?'

'I don't know.' I didn't know, that was the maddening thing. I said, 'Maybe they were all opened by the Queen Mother or designed by the same architect or something. *Anything* in common.'

Matson was looking at me curiously. 'Confidential?'

'Yes,' I said. 'Confidential. But I'm afraid there's no money in it.'

'Pity.' He smiled slightly. Maybe he'd thought I was on to some kind of a deal. 'I'll run these through the computer and see what it comes up with.'

'Thanks.' I said. 'I'd be grateful.'

'Feel like a nightcap?'

Not even for the use of his computer did I feel like a nightcap. I shook my head. 'Nice of you, but I'm off home.'

But I wasn't, because there was Sid Walker buttonholing me.

'A word in your ear, Mr Straun?'

Well, he might have been about to offer the skeleton of Henry the Fifth's charger or something. Greed makes fools of us all.

'Yes, Mr Walker?'

'Perhaps the office?'

Well, all right, the office, but it had better be good. God, but I was tired. Sid led the way, shut the glass door and produced brandy. After pouring he said, 'Ever use floating golf balls, Mr Straun?'

To most people it would have sounded a bit out of character with Sid Walker, through whose salerooms passed some of the most price-fetching golf memorabilia in the country. I happened to know that he'd sold a couple of featheries for two thousand pounds apiece only the week before, so I sipped my Rémy Martin and said, 'No. I'm told Americans use them sometimes because they have more water hazards than we do.'

'Not very common over here, then?'

'No indeed.' More curiosities than anything. Bill Tilling's shop had advertised them, but then Thetfield had its lake. I said, 'Why do you ask?'

Sid swirled brandy round his glass. He said, 'My youngest boy's a great golfer.'

'Is he?' I said. 'I didn't know that.' I hadn't, either. But then there was precious little I did know about the family Walker after hours. I hadn't even known he was married, come to that.

'Oh yes,' Sid told me. 'Great golfer. Proper mad on it, he is. He's the one that keeps his eye open for the old stuff. The Victorian clubs and that.'

I'd wondered where he got it from, something to be learned every day. I asked, 'Where does your boy play?'

'Little Marling. Out Aylesbury way.'

I put my glass down. 'Oh yes?'

'Some kids offered my Len these balls. Said they'd found them. All brand new they was.' Sid Walker paused. 'Len asked if I was interested, but of course they ain't antique. Not a thing for me at all, but I thought you might be interested.'

'That was a kind thought, Mr Walker,' I said. 'Very kind indeed. Does your son happen to know how these children came by these balls?'

'Found them, Mr Straun,' Sid said. 'The kids found them

floating on the water in one of those old gravel pits they've got out there. Say that more keep popping up each day. Funny, innit?'

CHAPTER 10

Myers from Aylesbury had got all the gear ready by the time I arrived at Little Marling. Road diversion signs were in place and the crane on the big recovery truck swung out over the water that filled the old gravel workings. The diver had already gone down and hooked up to whatever was down there in the murk and the steel cable was vibrating under the strain like a fishing line on to a big catch. We'd stood around in a little group, listening to the whine of the crane's motor and the cross noises of the local birds who resented being disturbed at that hour in the morning. The pit must have been deep because it seemed an age before the rear bumper of the Ford Transit showed, but after that it came up quick enough. We'd waited until the water had stopped spouting out of a broken window and then gone over to have a look.

'All very satisfactory,' Myers had said.

The missing golf gear was in the back, and there were a lot of loose balls about, the floaters had obviously escaped through the broken window. I checked on the tyres but I knew this was the Constantines' van without looking. It's not easy to fake an alibi with people because unless you're lucky enough to have an identical twin, people are always different. But much easier to duplicate a van, as Stephanos must have realized. One in the police pound and another on the road. On second thoughts, it didn't sound much like Stephanos. Far more likely to be Rosa. 'If it's all right with you,' I told Myers, 'we'll keep news of the van to ourselves for the moment. I know the villain who owns it and I don't want him to take fright just yet.'

'You mean we keep a low profile,' said Myers, who was a chap who knew his Radio 4.

'Yes,' I said. 'A low profile. Held very close to the chest.'

It was in the air.

'Shouldn't bother to tell all this to Mr Todhunter,' Gareth Evans said when I'd broken the good news. 'No good clouding the water.'

'Right,' I said. 'Mum's the word.' I hadn't intended saying anything anyway.

'Funny thing to do, steal a load of stuff and then dump it in a pond.' Gareth Evans was doodling again. I didn't say anything, because it was past eleven and I wanted a cup of coffee before I started on my next assignment and I had a feeling it was going to be one of those days. I was right, because he added, 'When you've finished with Todhunter you might just call in at the Jehari Embassy on your way back. They rang up while you were out and asked to see an officer.'

I didn't like to give him the satisfaction but it took me a moment to react to that one. Finally I said, 'What about, for God's sake?'

'I didn't ask.' Gareth Evans looked me firmly in the eye. There was no getting away from the fact that there were times when you had to admire him. He glanced at the clock on the wall. 'You'd best be getting on, boyo. Have a nice day.'

Due to some kind of duty rota system, Monday was a Todhunter day of rest, which meant I was summoned to his home. I found him kneeling on his lawn, his knees cushioned against the proximity of the earth by a sponge rubber mat. Every now and then he stabbed at a weed with a stainless steel tool and dropped the resultant corpse into the trug standing ready at his side.

Taken from their normal environment most people undergo some sort of sea change, but apparently members of the Foreign Office don't conform. Todhunter was wearing a houndstooth hacking jacket, whipcord trousers and green Derri boots for his agricultural chores but he managed to be exactly the same as the man who had briefed me in Gareth Evans's office. Even the full country gear for weeding the room-sized lawn behind a Georgian gem in Islington didn't look all that absurd.

Todhunter sat back on his haunches in much the same way as an Indian tonga-driver squats waiting for a fare, no mean feat, and looked up at me. 'You couldn't tell Jager anything about Freddy Wong that he didn't know already. So you had a wasted journey.'

I said yes, I had.

'Well, I'm sorry about that.' Todhunter didn't look particularly apologetic. 'But I wish I understood your feelings about Jager. All right, so he smashes a golf club in a fit of temper. Haven't you ever done the same?'

'No,' I said, 'I haven't.' A strong urge perhaps but not the whole hog. Not with clubs the price they are.

Todhunter said, 'Well I have.' He paused, possibly remembering the occasion but I didn't ask, and he went on, 'You don't seriously think that business in the—er, theatre was anything to do with Jager, do you? There must be plenty of rough stuff in places like that.'

I said, 'I saw him come out of the theatre. Nobody had roughed him up.'

'Nobody had roughed *you* up, either. Perhaps he can just take care of himself.'

'Well,' I said, 'I'd still like to know how the police managed to arrive so quickly. It was as though they'd been called *before* the trouble began.'

Todhunter bounced gently up and down, as though it helped his thinking. 'Suppose they had. What would be the point? What would they find?'

I said, 'They'd have found me engaged in what appeared to be a drunken brawl in a sex theatre. Maybe I'd have been stark naked in the middle of that bloody stage along with the resident act. I don't know. But if Jager wanted to discredit me it would be as good a way as any.'

'And why should he want to discredit you?'

I didn't know, and Todhunter knew damn well that I didn't know, not for certain. I said, 'He may think I'm asking too many questions.'

'About an unfortunate accident?'

I said doggedly, 'Perhaps. Or about the theft from the professional's shop.'

Perhaps he read more into my words than I'd intended. 'You're not suggesting that a millionaire industrialist would steal a few bits and pieces of golf equipment, surely?'

'I'm not suggesting anything,' I told him. 'I was just pointing out that within twenty-four hours Thetfield Golf Club has had more than its fair share of incidents of one sort or another. It could be just coincidence.'

'It could well be.' Todhunter didn't add that it had better be, because he didn't have to. He added, 'I understand Jager is friendly with your ex-wife.'

'Yes, he is.' Crafty sod, where had he dug that one from? Or, more to the point, who had done the digging for him? Evans Superintendent presumably, although I'd never mentioned Angela to him either, fool that I was. The old sad story of the English gent trying to keep the lady's name out of it.

Todhunter sighed. 'Forgive me, Inspector, but one has to allow for personalities. I don't know anything about the relationship between your ex-wife and yourself but I suppose it would be understandable if you resented a new association?'

I said, 'I wouldn't subject a man to harassment just because he was friendly with a woman I was once married to, if that's what you mean.'

'I'm sure you wouldn't.'

'Damn it,' I said, 'the only reason I got involved in this at all was because Angela asked me to. So far as I'm concerned she can marry Jager tomorrow.' But it was not entirely true. Angela marrying Jager would make him Sam's stepfather, and while Angela was entitled to do what she liked with her own life, Sam was something else again. No, my plans for my son's future did not include Dirk Jager.

Mrs Todhunter came out of the house carrying tea-things on a silver tray. She was a slim, well-groomed woman of perhaps forty; I wondered if she might be slightly older than her husband, but with a certain type of man and woman it's hard to tell. She put the tray down on the small, white-painted pierced iron table at my side and gave it a quick glance as though checking it out before smiling at me.

'I don't know if you like milk or lemon, Inspector, but if it's milk I'm afraid it's the long life stuff. Adrian and I like lemon and the cat adores long life, so consequently we're always running out of anything else.'

I said, 'I'm like the cat. I like long life, too.'

Mrs Todhunter smiled at me understandingly and went back inside the house. I got the impression that she was used to serving tea to people she didn't know and would probably never see again.

When his wife was out of earshot Todhunter poured the tea, handed me my cup and said, 'I'm glad you take that view of things and I'm sure there's absolutely no reason to think that Dirk Jager has been anything other than a model visitor to these shores. The least we can do is to see that he isn't harassed. Particularly by the police.'

I thought that one over. Finally I said, 'In other words, no further investigations involving Mr Jager.'

'Admirably put.' Todhunter put his cup down carefully. 'I'll even improve on it. Lay off Dirk Jager, Inspector. Totally. One hundred per cent. So far as HM Government is concerned, he's a welcome and potentially valuable guest and he stays that way.'

'And Freddy Wong?'

Todhunter frowned. 'The man's a thoroughgoing rogue and the sooner we see the back of him the better.'

I said, 'That's a bit difficult since he's got diplomatic immunity.'

'If you can make something stick we could tell the embassy he's *persona non grata*.'

I didn't say anything. We both knew that with the Jehari Embassy it wouldn't be as easy as that. If Wong had committed a nice gory murder it might be worth a try but I doubted if the average Jehari diplomat realized murder was illegal anyway.

I got back to the office about two to collect a car and see if there was anything on my desk. Gareth Evans was having an appointment with the Deputy Commissioner and nobody else seemed anxious to get involved in my troubles, something for which I'd normally have been grateful, but today I found it irritating. Why had it suddenly become my lot to cope with the Todhunters of this world?

'The Hunter inquest has been held over for Mr Jager's evidence,' my sergeant, Endicott, was saying. 'Do you want me to get you a sandwich?'

I didn't want a sandwich but if I had anything more ambitious for lunch the time would have to be made up later and I didn't fancy that. 'All right,' I said, 'a sandwich and coffee. What about Tilling? Have they come up with the post-mortem report yet?'

'Yes, sir.' Endicott shuffled papers. 'Seems he was dead before he was killed in the car. If you get my meaning.'

I got his meaning all right. But why? Even among people like the Constantines you didn't come to that sort of end for nothing. I thought of Winnie Tilling and wondered how she'd take the news. Does it make any difference if your husband is murdered or just died in a traffic accident? I didn't know. Sergeant Endicott brought my sandwich and I told him to lay on the car.

'Shall you be coming back, sir?'

A good question so far as the People's Republic of Jehar was concerned, because like the lion's cave in the fable, more footprints went in than came out.

'Don't wait up for me, Sergeant Endicott,' I said. 'But if I'm not back by dawn send in the troops.'

'Sir?'

'A joke, Sergeant,' I said. 'A joke.' But for all that I wasn't laughing.

The Jehari Embassy was up the top of Queensgate, a rather elegant confection from the Regency, with what estate agents like to call a good elevation. Its previous tenants had been a small South American republic who'd kept the whole thing rather well, a state of affairs that hadn't lasted. Presumably in an effort to show solidarity with the people, the place had developed the look of a long-term squat, which wasn't helped by political opponents of the regime spraying what were presumably rude messages in aerosol paint over the once white stonework. I told my constable driver to wait and tried to exude a little confidence as I marched up to the front door.

'Inspector Straun,' I announced. 'Mr Riza is expecting me.' According to well-informed sources, Ali Riza was First Secretary. The blue-chinned, haggard young man who had opened the door to me wore a turban over a rather nasty blue suit which bulged suggestively in front of his left shoulder. How he dressed in his own embassy was his affair but I hoped he'd get rid of what caused the bulge before setting foot in the street.

'Not here.'

I'd suspected it might be like this, so I persevered. Blue Chin went away and returned with a piece of paper, on which someone had scribbled *Bendall's Shooting Grounds*.

'Knowing?'

I said yes, I was knowing. They were beyond Hatfield on the A1, a centre for clay pigeon shooters and anyone trying guns. I asked doubtfully, 'Mr Riza will see me there?'

Blue Chin showed a lot of unexpectedly good teeth. 'Sure thing. Doctor Haziz buying guns. Always take First Secretary along.'

Running time to Hatfield was about half an hour and another ten minutes fetched us up at Bendall's, a stretch of one-time farmland saved somehow or other from development. There was a car park, a kind of club house, and a few people huddled together to one side of a clay launcher. I got out and went over to make myself known.

There's a mystique about the buying of first-class weaponry, ancient or modern. Ancient I knew about.

'The People's Ambassador wishes a pair of guns,' Ali Riza told me. He himself did not look like a First Secretary, he looked more like a forty-year-old Middle Eastern shopkeeper, dressed in cheap and creased Western clothes and, rather incongruously, the type of peaked cap made famous by Fidel Castro. His face was heavy-cheeked and his eyes brightly and cockily intelligent, like those of a giant blackbird. Haziz, on the other hand, was a lean, hard fifty-year-old with the bony face and mad eyes of a tortured priest. Apart from a conventional, loosely wound Arab headdress, he was wearing a kind of military combat jacket above whipcord slacks pushed into rubber boots while he inspected a shotgun in the hands of a formally dressed, grey-haired

English gent. Neither the People's Ambassador nor his
Secretary looked the kind of people customarily found at
the Court of St James.

The gun, a most beautiful double barrelled hammerless
twelve-bore, would have been welcome anywhere, though I
guessed you'd have to part with thirty thousand or so before
it would be yours to take along.

'Perhaps Your Excellency would care to try the stock for
size,' the man from the gunsmiths was saying. He was used
to fitting people to thirty grand's worth of gun, and usually
the preliminary work of sizing would have been carried out
at the back of the shop using a try gun. Evidently with Dr
Haziz this had not been the case. Nor was it going to be.

'Gimme some shells, eh?' said the People's Ambassador.

The silver-grey-haired gentleman in the well-cut suit may
have blinked—once—but if he did I missed it. He handed
over the magnificent gun and a couple of twelve-bore car-
tridges, which the Ambassador slammed into the breech as
though he'd done something like that before.

'Pull!'

There was the twang of the spring and a clay arced across
the sky. The sun seemed to jump to the Ambassador's
shoulder of its own accord and the report smacked out at
the same moment. The clay disintegrated into a puff of dust.

'Pull!'

Bang!

Another puff. The Ambassador took a couple more car-
tridges and appeared to notice me for the first time, which
was Riza's cue to say something rapidly in Arabic. Dr
Haziz nodded curtly, his eyes on mine. If this was just an
Ambassador, I found myself wondering, what was the head
fundamentalist back home like?

Ali Riza said in his remarkable bazaar English, 'The
Ambassador making official report of missing person. Our
damn Press Attaché Wong.'

I wondered if it was true that the British face doesn't reveal what's going on behind it. I hoped it was, because I'd have hated them to see all those alarm bells ringing. If Freddy Wong was missing it was pretty certain it was because he wanted to be, so what had he been up to now? More to the point, where was he missing *from*?

I took out a notebook. 'I see, sir. Could you describe the gentleman?' It was pure Dixon of Dock Green and I was rather proud of it. It took a certain amount of steam from the Jeharis, too. Collapse of foreign party in face of British *sang froid*. They exchanged a certain amount of Arabic before Riza returned to business.

'Full name, Frederick Wong. Naturalized Jeharian subject—'

It wasn't a bad description as descriptions go, though of course it lacked the more lurid bits of Freddy's early life, and it had a few extra details, such as his call and conversion to Islam, that were new to me. I wrote them all down dutifully and when the First Secretary paused for breath I put in a question of my own.

'Why exactly are you reporting this gentleman missing, sir?'

Riza frowned. 'Not in his flat. Not in his office. The man has altogether gone.'

I said, 'Couldn't he have decided to take a few days off?'

'No.' He didn't even bother to qualify that one. Apparently nobody in the Embassy took days off, end of subject.

'Possibly he had a disagreement with someone at the Embassy?' I tried to look tactful.

Riza turned down his mouth and glowered at me. 'Why should he have disagreement?'

The thing was taking on a certain Alice in Wonderland quality. I mean, how was I supposed to know? 'Perhaps some misunderstanding with a colleague?' I suggested.

The Ambassador muttered and I got the impression he was becoming impatient. Riza nodded and turned back to me. 'This Wong sold the People's Ambassador a worthless article. He—sold rights in a non-existent property at a high price. The People's Ambassador is very angry.'

It was hard to believe, but then almost anything a high-grade con man does takes some swallowing. I said, 'What kind of property?' Not that I had to ask, I knew.

'It was a garage.'

It made a change from golf clubs, I thought. Well, he'd got guts, had Freddy Wong. Or a death wish. I'm damned if I'd have had the nerve to try it on the People's Ambassador, not when he had eyes like that. I said, 'You wish to make a charge?'

Riza shook his head violently. 'Only find. No charge. Mr Wong enjoys a diplomatic immunity. You find and give him to us.'

The People's Ambassador spoke in English for the first time. 'We will deal with the matter domestically,' he said. He dropped the cartridge he was holding into the waiting breech.

'Pull!'

Bang!

He didn't miss.

CHAPTER 11

The Wong residence was in Gloucester Place, an upper bracket district of service flats, discreet hotels and accountants' offices close to Baker Street. The top-floor flat in what had once been someone's town house was quiet, and from the landing window you had a nice view of the traffic lights.

'All right,' I said to Sergeant Endicott, 'open her up.'

'Yes, sir.' He did his best to put his Policeman Plod face on it, but he'd been waiting to do this ever since he joined the Force. He wasn't bad at it, either, although if people insist on living without deadlocks it's a wonder they don't have half London coming in to borrow the loo. Along with his breaking-in course, Endicott must have got in a spot of mind-reading, too, because as he pushed the door open he said, 'You'd have thought the gentleman would have known better.'

'Why waste money on a rented flat?' Freddy obviously hadn't seen himself as a long-term tenant, but just the same I felt a twinge of disappointment. If Freddy had any really horrible skeletons he'd presumably have kept them some-where else. But then, a con man keeps his wares in his head. Well, we'd find out soon enough.

It was a well furnished place, and so it should have been for the money he'd have paid for it. There was a single bedroom, a large living-room and what the estate agents call the usual offices. The whole place was as neat as a woman would have kept it, unlike the cosy shambles that marks the home of the average man. But then, Freddy was polished and dapper himself, not difficult to see him doing the light domestic.

Sergeant Endicott was looking around him appreciatively and I didn't blame him, I wouldn't have minded the place myself. 'What are we looking for, sir?'

Good question, Sergeant. What indeed are we looking for? I said, 'I'm damned if I know. Like the man in the book said, I'll know it when I see it.'

The bathroom had only what you'd expect in it and a lingering hint of Eau Sauvage, the kitchen was surprisingly well stocked by someone with a taste for pasta, which also was hardly surprising. The bedroom wardrobe yielded several suits, odds and ends of clothing, no letters, nothing you'd give a second thought to. I did the drawers, the bed, mattress, as much carpet as would turn up, the backs of the Piper lithos on the walls.

I looked at Endicott. 'Well?'

'Wouldn't you expect there to be a suitcase somewhere, sir?'

Oh excellent Endicott, not just a hopeful face.

'Yes,' I said. 'One would. One would expect his shaving gear in the bathroom, too, but it isn't there. There's probably a suit and a few shirts missing too, and I can't see the sort of yellow slacks he was wearing when we played golf.' I couldn't see any golf clubs either, come to that, but people who live in London flats probably kept things like that in the club locker-room or the boot of the car. 'All right,' I said, 'so what do we conclude so far?'

'That he's pushed off somewhere of his own accord?'

'Yes,' I said, 'and so would I if I worked for the same man he does.'

I walked through into the living-room. There was a fair amount of drink in the G Plan cupboard, nothing in the drawers of the functional little desk, a virgin notepad on top. Well, anything worth taking would presumably have gone with him. And if there was going to be anything to link him with Dirk Jager what was it likely to be? There was an unexpectedly well stocked bookshelf. Odd, the arrogance with which one expects a man to be illiterate simply because he's a villain. Couldn't be further from the truth sometimes. I flicked through what looked like an almost complete set of Bruce Chatwin paperbacks, most of Eric Newby's travel books, Paul Theroux, John Masters and the short version of the new transcription of Pepys. For some reason, no less than four books on the Zeebrugge naval operation in 1918. Somehow I hadn't imagined Freddy as a World War I nut.

'Not what you'd expect, is it, sir?' ventured Endicott.

'No.'

'Maybe he was lonely in the evenings. Read anything.'

I said, 'Well, I can't imagine he had all that much in common with the lads back at the Embassy.' There were a number of hardbacks piled sideways on the narrow shelf and Endicott took the first one and held it up. *No Seat of Mars: Angus Straun.*

'Fan of yours, sir.'

'I don't suppose it'll save him,' I said, 'but it'll be a close run thing.' I cocked my head on one side to read the others. *London Since the Romans, London's River, The Great Wen, London Journey.* There were others but they'd been shelved back to front.

I said, 'Make a note of those titles.'

Sergeant Endicott grinned. 'Wasn't there some saying in the last war, sir? "Know your Enemy"?'

'I think there was,' I said. 'If there wasn't, there should have been.'

I went over the rest of the room pretty thoroughly, but it had the impersonal, empty feeling of a hotel. There was a picture with which Freddy had amused himself, sticking odd mementoes of visits into the edge of the frame. Plan of the Regent's Park Zoo. The Longleat Lions. A picture-postcard of Sherwood Forest, a painted aerial view of a city I recognized as Bath. Bath! What the hell was Freddy doing in Bath? Or Longleat, for that matter? Once again Sergeant Endicott got in on my thoughts.

'Proper little tourist, wasn't he, sir?'

'He was a Press attaché,' I said. 'Maybe he got invited to most of these places.' Maybe. I picked up the waste-paper basket and emptied it on the floor. Detectives in crime stories find some of their best clues in among the waste paper, and I wasn't too proud to learn from my betters. I smoothed out the crumpled envelopes of junk mail, offers of plants that would provide your garden with a riot of flowering ground cover, and shopping lists that consisted of rather old-maidish *½ stnd raisins, pk.las.verd., black olives,* each with a neat tick to signify a mission accomplished. Freddy Wong, I thought, would have made someone a wonderful wife. I unravelled a ball of paper and found myself with a sheet slightly larger than the rest, blank, apart from the heading.

Department of the Environment
12 Napton Terrace
London SW1

A straightforward sheet of government departmental headed notepaper. Which didn't feel quite right. I took it over to the window and gave the thing a second look, which told me it was a Xerox copy. I thought what a good job the latest machines did—apart from a few scratch lines here and there, it was easy to imagine that before the sheet got crumpled it must have looked something very like the real thing.

So what had Freddy wanted with the Department of the Environment? I looked down at the traffic in the street below where a taxi had stopped in the middle of the road to pick up a fare, then back to the sheet of paper again as though expecting it to tell me the part it played in the great celestial scheme of things, but it kept predictably silent. Given a blank sheet of anybody's headed paper, Freddy would have been totally unable to resist the temptation to put it to some unfortunate use. One's mind boggled as to what he'd do with something that was headed *Chancellor of the Exchequer*. I indulged myself with a daydream of Freddy altering the tax structure of Great Britain overnight in an attempt to bring off some kind of mega-coup on the world's stock markets. Only this wasn't a chance sheet of someone else's paper that had just happened to come into his possession. This was a photo copy which he'd presumably been at some pains to collect. The thing was hopelessly crumpled, as though Freddy had fisted it tight in his hand,

and I did my best to smooth it out a bit more. This time I could just make out something in pencil in the right-hand corner. *GREENHOUSE ONE.* And then more carefully, HAB/27B/CB 1725/99/KT.

I said, 'Only a civil servant could invent a reference number like that.' In a manner of speaking. Some of our departmental stuff was just as tortuous but I understood those.

'The first group's the originator, the second the Branch Folder Number and the third's a reference, if any, to Central Registry.' Endicott frowned in concentration. 'I think the next one is a key to any relevant committee and the last one's the secretary who took it down. Sir.'

Well, that would teach me to keep my big mouth shut. Nevertheless I'd asked and he'd told me, so there couldn't be much wrong with that. I said, 'How the devil do you know that?'

'My sister's in the Environment Office, as a matter of fact. She's a clerical officer.'

'Is she now?' I said. '*Is* she!'

Endicott said cheerfully, 'Yes, sir. Her name's Doris.'

'Doris Endicott?'

'No, sir. Doris Soames. She's married.'

I said, 'Do you suppose it would embarrass your sister if she had a visit from the law?'

Sergeant Endicott grinned. 'I shouldn't think so, sir. Her husband's a VAT Inspector with Customs and Excise.'

Doris Soames was a nice lass with a bright smile and the same kind of tail-wagging look as her brother. She came downstairs to see us in the sort of anonymous waiting-room beloved of government departments and used her clerical officer's authority to get us a cup of tea and a sweet biscuit apiece, proving as ever that it's who you know that counts.

She took my smoothed-out sheet of paper and gave it a quick glance.

'Yes, Inspector, that's a photo copy of a sheet of the paper we use here. Would you like to see some of the original?'

'No,' I said. 'I'll take your word for it. What about this reference number? Any chance of your being able to tell which department it came from?'

She took a bit longer over that once. Finally she said, 'Would it be all right if I checked with Central Registry?'

'Yes,' I told her. 'Go ahead.'

'They're not all that quick. If I were you I'd have another cup of tea.'

She was right, but she came back eventually with a slightly puzzled look on her face.

'I'm sorry, but this doesn't mean a thing to anybody.' She gave me back the Xerox. 'It's funny because it *looks* like the kind of reference we use here. The right number of headings and the position of the originator's initials and so on. It's just that the numbers don't bear any relation to *anything*.'

I stood up. 'Well, thanks, Mrs Soames. We enjoyed the tea anyway.'

'If I have any bright ideas I'll let you know.'

I had one last shot. 'Suppose a member of the public wrote to the Department of the Environment. Would there be any kind of centralized way of checking?'

Doris Soames frowned. 'It would depend how he addressed the letter. I mean, if he was writing about pollution and he addressed it to something like "Pollution Department, Department of the Environment", then that's where it would go. The department would have a record, of course, but if you didn't know which department, it would be an almost impossible job. There are so many, you see.'

'Yes,' I said. 'I do indeed see. But thanks again for your help.'

Back at Tiverton House, Endicott said hopefully, 'Sir, couldn't we make some kind of guess at the department he might have written to?'

I said, 'Not really. He'd have taken something out of the blue. It wouldn't have mattered a damn what he wrote or who he wrote to just so long as it was something that called for an acknowledgement.' He looked at me politely, so I went on, 'I'm guessing that Freddy Wong just wanted a sheet of the Environment people's headed paper.'

Endicott said logically, 'But it would have had writing on it, sir.'

Well, yes, it would and here we went into the realms of fantasy. But then Freddy lived in that kind of world, so one might as well have a wild guess here and there. 'Look,' I said, 'all we know for certain about all this is that Frederick Wong makes his living out of spinning wild stories to people who are gullible enough to fork out on the strength of them. Right?'

'Right, sir.'

'So,' I said, 'it's bloody obvious that the more official-looking your sales pitch is, the better it will go down with the paying customer. Suppose you were a con man trying to flog a block of flats. What kind of tool would you need to make one hundred per cent sure your mug would bite?'

'Something that would suggest apartments were better than houses, I suppose, sir,' Sergeant Endicott hazarded. Then he grinned. 'Oh yes, I *see*, sir! Something official. Something like a leaked memo from No. 11—'

'Something like a Xeroxed leaked memo.' But he'd got the point all right. I had hopes of young Endicott.

Then his face fell. 'I still don't get the blank photo copy, though.'

I said, 'Suppose Wong got back a formal acknowledgement to some nonsense letter he wrote. Suppose he put a sheet of plain paper over the typing, then he could Xerox the two together and come up with a plain sheet of paper apart from the heading.' I added, 'As a matter of fact, I know he did that because we can still see the faint scratch of a line where the sheet overlapped. In practice it wouldn't show because Freddy would then lay his own phoney memo on top and re-Xerox the two together. That way he'd end up with what would look exactly like a Xerox copy of a departmental memo.'

'I say,' Sergeant Endicott said, 'that's pretty smart!' I waited for him to say who was the smarter, Freddy Wong or me, but he didn't. Instead he asked, 'And the reference number?'

I said, 'Well, he'd make that up, wouldn't he? He'd have a model of the kind of reference they use—he'd just have to invent one that looked much the same, only using made-up numbers. That's why your sister couldn't trace it.'

Endicott nodded. He really was a most appreciative audience. To every man his Sancho Panza. Finally he asked, 'So what was the memo that Freddy Wong made up?'

'Christ!' I said. 'I don't know. The fact that he did make one up will have to do for now.'

I sought out the Super and put the case to him.

'It isn't as if we knew who he was trying to con, it could have been anybody.' I held up the photocopy memo. 'As a way of showing how he works, this is great, but it's of no earthly practical use.'

Gareth Evans shrugged his shoulders. 'It's neither here nor there now, is it? We've got the Jehari Ambassador after his blood, and you know what that lot are like. Once they lay hands on Wong, he's for the chop—he knows it, too. That's why he's gone to ground. Mr Todhunter's been on the phone. There is to be no ambassadorial gun play in London, and that's official. So find the bloody man before the boys from Jehar do the job for you.'

I said, 'The Ambassador has made it clear that once

we find him he's to be handed over to them. Diplomatic immunity.'

'Bugger diplomatic immunity!' Gareth Evans could be very chapel when he chose. 'Wong's a cheeky little Yank con man who deserves to have his arse kicked, but he's no more a Jehari than you or I. Todhunter says to get hold of him and smuggle him out of the country while the going's good.'

I said, 'Well, at least it's practical—'

'Cause a war, too, if it's found out. Get cracking.'

I went back to my desk and sat there, staring out of the window. The light was beginning to go and great clouds of starlings were beginning to circle the West End, the lucky first million or so getting the prime roosting places at the back of the National Gallery. Even through the glass you could hear their steady, high yelling. Hard to like starlings. What was the saying? *Decent birds hop, rotten birds walk.* Starlings walked. But then, they would, wouldn't they? If you were a starling on the run, I thought, you'd be safe enough in that lot. What's one starling—

I said, 'Chinatown.'

The WPC who had just brought me a cup of coffee looked at me curiously. 'It's a film, sir. With Faye Dunaway. Years back now.'

'The place, Brown. The place.'

She looked hurt. Well, understandable. She hadn't signed on to do history, after all. 'I don't think there is a Chinatown any more, sir. It used to be the Chinese quarter in Limehouse, I believe. But that must have been before World War I.'

I said, 'Yes—the only Chinese community of any size in London is round Denman Street, in Soho.' But it seemed reasonable enough. If you were a Chinese on the run, you'd be less conspicuous if you lived among other Chinese. At a quick glance, they all look the same to us. On the other hand, I couldn't exactly visualize Freddy Wong bedding down with a lot of counter hands from Chinese takeaways. And if he did, he'd get knifed for conning them out of their life savings—

'My God!' I said aloud. 'That's it!'

'Sir?'

I said, 'Get a pencil. I want to know about every con job that's reported in the Met area from now until further notice.'

To expect Freddy Wong to live without shaking somebody down was like asking an alcoholic to live without a drink. Sooner or later someone was going to complain about being done. Or would he? If he didn't, London was the hell of a big place in which to look for one man.

CHAPTER 12

Form 126/b

Inter Office Memorandum

From: Chief Insp. Deedes, Warmsley Rd. E.

To: Insp. A. Straun, CID Tavistock House

Further to telephone call of 7th inst. it is confirmed that I received a complaint at 1432 hrs, which suggested a confidence fraud was being attempted. (Inter Station Memo. 732/AS/F refers.)

Information laid by a Mr K. V. Ramakrishnapillai, native of Sri Lanka, a visitor to UK resident at the Ritz Hotel, Piccadilly. Mr K.V.R. is a wealthy film producer, owning studios in India and Sri Lanka (millionaire?) and a world figure in sailing circles. At present trying to purchase a large sailing vessel in good condition and placed an advertisement to this effect in the personal columns of *The Times*.

This advertisement was answered by telephone. Call was

answered by Mrs K.V.R., whose English is not as good as that of her husband (educated Harvard University, USA). According to Mrs K.V.R., the caller offered a £10,000 option on a 3-masted clipper-rigged composite of 921 tons. The vessel was in good condition, 212 ft long and with a beam of 36 ft, built by Scott and Linton in 1869. Present owners: Unnamed consortium, who wish sale to be handled discreetly. Mr X has been nominated as negotiator.

Viewing: Discretion imperative, owing to American interest. If interested, Mr K.V.R. should board 11.0 a.m. water bus at Westminster Bridge, where he will be joined by Mr X. At this stage, only viewing at a discreet distance possible.

Station note: It would seem that in this case the con man chose the wrong punter. Although possessed of an attractively foreign name, Mr K.V.R. is clearly sophisticated and westernized, and highly knowledgeable on the subject of sailing ships, many of which he can readily identify from their bare dimensions. When laying his complaint Mr K.V.R.'s opening words were: 'Some son of a bitch is trying to sell me the *Cutty Sark*!'

CHAPTER 13

The *Cutty Sark*. A tea clipper from the great days of sail, dry-docked for ever like the USS *Constitution* or HMS *Victory* as national memorials to the way ships used to be, jealously guarded by learned societies and preserved by government-funded craftsmen, regardless of cost.

I thought about a con man offering her for sale to someone with a funny name. A name so odd that he might be presumed not to know that the *Cutty Sark*'s keel was stuck for ever in concrete at Greenwich Reach. I didn't laugh. If an old-time con man could sell the Eiffel Tower twice in one day, a modern one was certainly equal to flogging the *Cutty Sark*. The fact that Mr Ramakrishnapillai really knew about boats had been sheer bad luck. You win some, you lose some, it's the vision behind the pitch that counts. The sheer bloody excitement of making the outrageous sound plausible.

It could only be Freddy Wong, I thought. You really would have to be a compulsive con man to try this one. But I knew I was talking myself into it. London was stiff with con men who'd sell the Pyramids, the Lincoln Memorial and the Leaning Tower of Pisa as a special cut-price package if they thought they'd found the right man. No, I hadn't a thing to go on except that elusive sixth sense one calls a hunch. This one just smelled right. For my money there wasn't a chance of it being anyone else. God damn it, this had to be Wong.

There are worse ways of going downstream from Westminster than by water bus. You walk down a flight of stone steps that lead from the Victoria Embankment and find yourself at a small berth, complete with ticket office and waiting-room. For about 50 pence a stage the square built, double-decker vessel transports you as far as Greenwich with a minimum of fuss and a good deal quicker than you'd expect. It was new to me and I was impressed and said as much to Sergeant Joseph Endicott.

'Londoners have been getting about this way for hundreds of years, sir. Before the seventeenth century, it was just about the only way.' The gentle condescension of the native for the stranger. Well, why not? It was his city and proud of it.

Beneath us the diesel chuckled and we slid away out into the grey Thames while I watched the embankment drift by. Trees and Charing Cross Station, the vast grey mass of the

Adelphi complex, Shell Mex House and the elegant tiered windows of the Savoy.

It was Joe Endicott's first day out in plain clothes. Rather a nice Donegal tweed, too, and he was a good-looking lad. I asked him how it felt.

He grinned. The usual effective show of good teeth against a dark face. 'Pretty good, sir. Though I'm not sure what you want me for.'

I said, 'I want you as a stand-in for Mr Ramakrishnapillai. Whoever this joker is who's selling our national heritage is going to be put off if he can't see him. Soon as we get to Greenwich your job is to stand well away from me and look rich.'

Endicott frowned. 'Don't I look a bit young, sir?'

'Yes,' I admitted, 'you do. But he won't spot that until he's safe aboard.'

He still looked doubtful. 'But, sir—I looked Sri Lanka up. I reckon Ramakrishnapillai's a Tamil, and they're a lot darker than us Jamaicans.'

I said patiently, '*You* know that, Joe, and so do I. But I very much doubt if Freddy Wong does.'

'I hope you're right sir,' Joe said resignedly.

Well, yes, I hoped so, too. But it was all right sitting in the sun, ticking off the sights like a tourist. Cleopatra's Needle, the *Discovery*, Blackfriars Bridge . . .

By Deptford most of our fellow passengers had gone. Endicott leaned over the rail aft and took photographs of the river bank, while I sat as far away as possible with my back to him. I heard footsteps coming up the steps to the upper deck.

'Good morning, sir. Mr Ramakrishnapillai?' The easy admiration one feels for other people's gifts. With my back to them it was almost impossible not to believe that the speaker wasn't a rather earnest banker from Boston. He certainly didn't sound like my chipper friend from Mineola but he was, he was.

'No, I am not Mr Ramakrishnapillai,' Sergeant Endicott's voice was his own. 'And you're nicked.'

I stood up and turned round. Diplomatic immunity being what it is, he couldn't really be nicked but Joe had got a kick out of saying it, so why not? It put a message over, if nothing else.

'Hello, Freddy,' I said. 'Sold any good garages lately?'

'Oh, shit.' He was a good loser. He'd gone to the trouble of dressing himself up for the part in a charcoal grey suit, a cream shirt and a plain black knitted silk tie. The briefcase he held probably contained no more than the morning paper but the effect was flawless. You'd have to be a policeman not to buy a boat from him.

I said, 'You picked the wrong man in Mr Ramakrishnapillai, Freddy.' I nodded towards the shore. 'Shall we get off and have a talk?'

The Chinese are supposed to be inscrutable, and Freddy, half Chinese, showed what I took to be a certain wary confidence. He said easily, 'Sure we can have a talk. But like I said the other day, there's no way you can book me. Not without starting a war or whatever.'

'Who said anything about booking you?' I did my best to look surprised at the thought, the ham actor in the best of us. 'No, we're just taking you back to your Embassy. Once we've handed you over, that's it.'

He really needed his Chinese half on that one. I saw his dark eyes blink once, then he'd recovered himself. 'What's with this handing over? You people acting as some kind of collection agency?'

I said, 'We've been asked to find you, Freddy. Whether we do or not is up to you.'

He nodded. 'OK. We'll get off at Charlton, then we talk.' He hesitated. 'Anyone from the Embassy know you're here?'

'No.'

'You weren't followed?'

'Not unless someone was chasing along the Embankment on a bicycle,' I told him. 'There were no Middle Eastern gentlemen on board with us at any time, and you can see there aren't any now.'

He nodded, looking relieved, but as we chugged on down river I could see he was edgy. I said, 'Has London run out of old ladies, that you've got to try your luck with your Jehari chums?'

For the first time I thought he looked dispirited. 'Win some, lose some,' he observed. 'It seemed a good idea at the time.'

'Back in Jehar,' Sergeant Endicott said unexpectedly, 'people get their hands cut off for charging *interest*.'

Freddy Wong blinked again. 'They do?'

'Yes,' I said, 'don't you know anything at all about Islamic fundamentalists?'

'I'm beginning to.'

I said unsympathetically, 'Well, you'd better start thinking about what they'll cut off a chap who sells them a non-existent garage. Interest may be out, but Islam is strong on the profit motive.'

We got off at Charlton.

'I've got a car,' Freddy said. 'We'll go to my place.' I could see by the way he looked around that he wasn't going to be happy until he was under cover.

Joe Endicott asked him why he hadn't parked his car back at Woolwich, where he'd got on the ferry.

'Because I wanted the guy with the long name to see the old boat from the river.' Freddy looked hurt. 'Hell, I couldn't lelt him see it from the *land*. The thing's floating in concrete.'

I said, 'I still don't understand how you thought Rama-krishnapillai would never have heard of the *Cutty Sark*.' I wasn't niggling the man. I genuinely wanted to know.

'I don't see why he *should* have heard of it,' Freddy said

sourly. 'I hadn't.' He slowed his steady march along the pavements. 'My car.'

Not strictly true, unless he'd won it off them in a poker game. It was the Constantines' pink Rolls. So Freddy knew the Constantines. So had Tilling. I wondered who else moved in that select circle.

'Yours?' I wanted to hear what he would say.

'Some chance. I got lent it by a friend to give the boat business a bit of class.'

I doubted if I'd risk buying a boat off a man who drove a pink Roller, but then, it takes all sorts. Endicott and I got in and we drove east. We passed Charlton Station. The Constantines had a more or less legitimate scrap metal business in these parts, I remembered. Acres of old cooking stoves and refrigerators gutted and squashed into cubes ready to be floated away somewhere in lighters, presumably to be recycled into the same thing all over again. Why did a man become a villain when he had it in him to be a successful and legitimate businessman? The same reason, presumably, that makes nice men cheat on their nice wives and vice versa, the built-in bloody mindedness of life.

Freddy parked in a desolate side-street and we walked between used car lots and half-derelict buildings where men did things with blow torches. It hadn't rained for days, but underfoot the street was full of puddles and patches of grease, so that the water that sloshed over one's shoes wore a rainbow sheen of oil. Here and there an optimistic council had left a skip in the gutter and they'd been filled with junk and never emptied, so that filthy paper and plastic packing lay soaking in mud or hung, caught by the wind, against the torn wire mesh that separated one enterprise from the next. I wondered what had brought about this appalling wasteland. German bombs? I thought bleakly that World War II was nearly half a century ago, and even we should have got around to something since then. But presumably if you wanted a patch on which to cut up old bedsteads, this was where it came cheap.

At the end of the road there was a huddle of real buildings, like a freak block that had survived in a nuked city. There was a riverside warehouse made over into apartments, a desolate Victorian pub and, facing them, a pie and chips café and the kind of basic corner shop that sells bread and baked beans, with a corner for video rental and condoms behind the counter.

At the warehouse Freddy stopped and said, 'I've got a place here.'

'Fine,' I said. 'We'll talk there.'

He looked at me, probably wondering what his chances were. 'Sure I'll talk. Only—how about just the two of us?'

It was unlikely he planned to attack me with some deadly martial art, and rightly or wrongly I didn't see him trying to bribe me. Probably it was curiosity as much as anything else that prompted me to agree. 'All right.' To Sergeant Endicott I said, 'Try the caff for a cup of coffee, Joe. Sit in the window so you can see if I need help.'

Endicott grinned. 'I don't think Mr Wong is planning anything silly.' He looked down at him. 'Are you, sir?'

'I just want a word in private, for Chrissake.' Freddy was edgy. None of that oriental calm this afternoon, and no wonder, with a pack of Dr Haziz's hit men after his guts.

Endicott opened the back door and got out, leaving Freddy and me alone.

I looked up at the warehouse, one of those once-derelict buildings that would now be got up within an inch of its life. 'Borrowed this off a friend, too?' I asked.

'No chance.' Freddy showed no eagerness to get out. 'I rented it off an agency.'

'You're *paying* for it?' A twinge of admiration for Islamic fundamentalism. For him to have actually paid good money for a bolt hole, Freddy must have been hard pressed indeed.

He said sourly, 'Sure I'm paying for it. So would you, if you'd seen what I've seen. Like an ambassador who sleeps with a machine pistol.'

I said, 'They're your people, Freddy. Your country. You're the all-Jeharian boy now.'

Freddy took a duster from the glove pocket and rolled it carefully into a ball. To everyone his security blanket. 'Look,' he said, 'I got myself in one hell of a fix last year.'

I said yes, I knew how it was, although I didn't and in no way did I want to.

Freddy unrolled his duster and started making it into a square. He said, 'It was pretty easy, making myself useful. Half the Jehari top men can't speak English—some can't even read and write. They sent me over here because they needed someone like me to handle the media bit, and when I saw it would get me diplomatic immunity I jumped at the chance. Hell, who wouldn't?' I didn't answer that one. We looked at each other. 'Look,' Freddy said, 'I'll level with you. What are the chances of you helping me? I got to get back to the States.'

I said brutally, 'You aren't an American citizen any more. They won't let you in.'

'Jesus . . .' I think for the first time it began to dawn on him just what he'd done, just how deep the hole he'd dug.

'There's nothing to stop you leaving the country,' I told him. 'The problem will be finding some country that will let you in. I don't imagine anywhere in Europe is going to accept a Jeharian national without at least a visa, and getting one can be tricky.' I let that sink in for a bit and then added, 'Though it's just possible I might be able to help.'

Freddy put down his duster. It was one of those moments when most people in his position would have been looking hopeful but Freddy had spent most of his life thinking one thing while looking another and the trick wasn't going to leave him now. Instead he said, 'What's the deal?'

'For a start,' I said, 'you could tell me what kind of a deal you were selling Jager.'

'I wasn't selling anything to Jager.' More reflex than an answer. He looked out of the window at the warehouse and the grey river washing past beyond. 'We just played golf together. You know how it is.'

'You've never just played golf for the fun of it in your life,' I told him. 'Remember that day we played together at Thetfield? You were setting me up before we'd played for more than a couple of holes.'

Freddy sighed. 'OK. So I was trying to sell him the same thing I tried with you. The garage one, remember?'

'The Japanese golf club was me,' I told him. 'Jager got something else. Let's start with a forged memorandum from the D of E. And if you want anyone to help you keep out of the way of your fellow diplomats, I suggest you keep to the point.'

Freddy turned back from the window. His eyes weren't wide because they weren't built that way but he looked as surprised and as wary as I imagine he was ever likely to be. He said softly, 'Who in hell told you about that?'

I said, 'Look, I know how you got yourself a sheet of headed Government paper and I know the mechanics of how you cooked up what looked like a leaked ministerial communication. What I don't know is what it was supposed to be about. Tell me.'

'You feel like a drink?'

I shook my head. 'Get on with it, Freddy. I've got plenty of time, but you haven't.'

He grimaced at that, then nodded. 'OK. You've heard of the greenhouse effect?'

'Who hasn't?'

'So everyone's heard of it. Now suppose someone comes

LAID DEAD 141

to you one day and says that he's got a good friend in a government office. This friend has come across a secret document that's code-named Greenhouse One and it worries her very much. She's very environmentally conscious, you see. As a matter of fact she's so damn conscious that she sneaks a copy of Greenhouse One and brings it out. And what does it say?'

'Exceptionally high tides due to the melting ice cap threaten London?'

Freddy looked upset. 'How in hell did you know that?'

'I didn't know it,' I said. 'Call it an informed guess. So you told Dirk Jager that the Thames was going to flood. What then?'

'I said I knew of some property I could buy cheap down towards Gravesend,' Freddy said sulkily.

'Why that far out?'

'Because it isn't to flood west of the Thames flood barrier, is it?' He'd obviously done his homework.

'So?'

'So I said we could get an option on the property and then insure it heavily. Then when it *did* flood we'd cash in.'

I damn nearly said 'but it wasn't going to flood anyway' but stopped myself just in time. The age-old problem of sorting the fact from the fiction. I said, 'So you stood to make—'

'The money he advanced for the option,' Freddy finished for me. 'And the insurance premium.'

'How much?' It wasn't idle curiosity. I was fascinated.

'About twenty grand.'

I said, 'You're not going to tell me that you thought someone like Jager would fall for a story like that—'

'Fall for it!' Freddy's voice rose querulously. 'Fall for it? There was no stopping him.' He paused. 'You'd better come upstairs. I want to show you something.'

I opened my door and swung my feet over the Rolls's

pink sills to the ground. I think Freddy must have stayed to put his duster back in the glove pocket or something because I was already standing by my open door before he started to open his. I saw Freddy's body black against a sudden blinding white light, then the force of the explosion crashed in on my senses as it picked me up and threw me endlessly through time and space until I hit something a million miles away and I sank gratefully into endless dark.

CHAPTER 14

I had forgotten that there was so much difference between fictional violence and the real thing. A long time ago I'd found out for myself but it had been a very long time ago, and I'd got into the way of thinking that the books had got it right. That you really did open your eyes to find yourself tucked up in a nice white hospital bed, lying there drowsily and staring at the ceiling until slowly the face of a beautiful woman came into focus.

You muttered, 'Where am I?' and the woman would cry, 'Oh thank God! Thank God!' while tears of joy began to stream down her face. This time it wasn't like that. I woke up with my face in the gutter and the first thing of which I was conscious was pain, closely followed by a gut terror that I was going to suffocate in my own blood. The pain was of the kind that had me on both counts—an overall racking of what seemed to be every nerve end in my body, a sheer physical agony that was made worse by dread of what was causing it. How much damage had been done to me? At such times the true Brit grits his teeth and does his best not to let the side down, and the noise I made had nothing to do with me, but simply came out of its own accord. It must have started as a scream or a yell but it ended as a rather disgusting gargle. Who would have thought the old man had so much blood in him? *Macbeth*. I didn't have to spit the stuff out, I just opened my mouth.

'Bloody hell!' Joe Endicott's voice was somewhere above me and I felt his hands clamp under my arms and haul me upright. Joe's hands were West Indian, café-au-lait-coloured, narrow, with fingers about ten inches long that looked as though they'd been designed to wrap round the fingerboard of a guitar. Which maybe they were, but they gripped me like steel hooks just the same. He said urgently, 'Anything bust, man?'

I said, 'I'm all right.' I was still playing John Mills in a black and white film, but the words didn't come out the way I intended. Being upright wasn't all that good because the blood from wherever it was started to find its way down my throat. It didn't agree with me and I threw up messily over the front of my jacket.

I said, 'Oh Christ!' in disgust and passed out again. It was a sequence that was to be repeated on and off for what seemed a long time before Joe got me with my head pillowed in his coat and from there into an ambulance and finally into the Mile End Hospital where they gave me something that mercifully knocked me out all over again.

When I came out of that little lot I was alone in a small white and green room painted in a style that wouldn't have been unfamiliar to Florence Nightingale. No lovely lady by my bedside, although eventually a nurse came through the door carrying some kind of stainless steel container. She was very black, and as she was smiling, her teeth showed like some kind of advertisement for fluoride. She was evidently a girl who knew what she was about because the stainless steel thing came in useful when I was promptly sick in it.

'Thass all right, luv,' said Florence Nightingale in the authentic accents of East London. 'Feel better now?'

For lo, thou art black but comely. She was a nice girl and I didn't want to disappoint her. 'Yes,' I said; it came out 'Yeth'. My tongue seemed to be painful along with the rest of me and twice its size. Also there were things stuck over my nose. Also my head felt as if it was about to split open. I steeled myself and muttered, 'What's wrong with my mouth?'

A bearded young man in a white coat came in carrying a clipboard. He said shortly, 'You bit your tongue. Won't improve your speech for a bit but it'll be all right.'

I said tentatively, 'Nose?'

'Broken. No problem.' He eyed me with professional interest. 'You were in an explosion. Do you remember?'

I nodded. I remembered all right.

'That's good.' He looked relieved. 'So far as we can make out, you tried to push your way through a car door. You didn't succeed, of course.'

I concentrated hard on my tongue and managed to ask what else was wrong.

'Concussed. Extensively bruised. Black and blue, as they say. But nothing else broken, though I can't imagine why not. You're lucky to be alive, come to that.' He was almost chatty all of a sudden, pleased, I suppose, to be the bearer of good news for once. I had never wanted to be a doctor.

'What about the other chap?'

He frowned. 'Friend of yours?'

I shook my head incautiously. Oh dear. Florence Nightingale moved swiftly to my side with her useful gadget, and just as well.

'That'll pass,' the doctor said as I was being mopped up. 'There's not much left of the other chap, whoever he was. To put it crudely, they're scraping him off the walls.' He prodded around me for a while, so I asked him how long I was likely to enjoy his company. 'Three or four days. You won't be up to much, though.'

I believed him. I asked him if there was a police officer about but he said no. There had been a West Indian in plain clothes who'd waited for several hours but when it was clear I was going to be all right he had been recalled. 'That all right?'

'Oh yes,' I said. 'That's fine.' I shut my eyes and thought kindly of Joseph Endicott. Kindly, too, in a curious way, of Freddy Wong. You bring nothing into this world and it is certain that you take nothing out of it. That wouldn't appeal much to Freddy, I thought, that amiable rogue. I hoped he'd be able to bluff his way into whatever paradise there is for con men. A sort of fraudulent Valhalla, with the revellers recounting for ever the time they sold little for much—

The doctor and the nurse went away and left me alone to doze. I had no idea of time, but I knew that if the doctor said I'd be fit to leave hospital in three or four days the chances were I could manage it a good deal quicker. I remembered how injured cats sometimes sit for ever without moving while they let themselves mend and I tried to compose myself to do the same. I even forced my mind to make itself a blank, every now and then I suppose I opened my eyes, only to shut them again.

Someone said, 'Angus.'

It was an effort to get my eyelids up but I made it, and this time fact had caught up with fiction. There really was a beautiful woman looking down at me, and with a further effort I got her face into focus. A fair-haired girl with big horn-rimmed glasses, whose name I'd remember any moment now.

I made an effort and out it came. 'Hello.' Not much but the best I could manage in the circumstances.

'Oh, you stupid bastard,' Laurie said. 'I knew this would happen.'

She bent down to kiss me and though she'd got her lines wrong I could see the tears running down her face.

Things were a good deal better next day, and when she came again I was almost human. She was wearing a light green dress made of some kind of linen stuff and I found msyelf thinking how beautiful she was. Odd, the in-built bloody-mindedness of the human male, which I'd sworn to guard against.

'Did you bring the map?'

Yes, she said, she'd brought the map I'd asked for. 'I got it from that place in Long Acre.'

'Show me.' It was still difficult to talk but I managed to, somehow. She unfolded it on the table beside my bed. I asked, 'Did you mark the place?'

'The ones Jager had marked in his road map? Yes.' Laurie held the map up so that I could see it. It was a hefty scaled thing, with clearly marked contours. She'd marked Jager's properties with a red felt-tipped pen, and it took only a second for me to read the contours.

I said, 'It doesn't make any kind of sense.' Seen on a decent map I realized that it could never have made sense, because the properties weren't near enough to the river, but one can draw some pretty daft conclusions first time around.

Laurie took the map from me. 'Why not?'

I said, 'The whole point of Freddy Wong's con was that Jager should buy buildings that would be threatened by Greenhouse One and make a killing on the insurance. The buildings Jager has got marked simply wouldn't be threatened by a flood—they're well away from any danger area. And they're on comparatively high ground anyway.'

'So they're something entirely different.' There was a touch of impatience in Laurie's voice and I couldn't blame her. She folded the map up crisply. 'Didn't you say that Jager made a lot of his money developing property?'

'Yes.'

'Well, there you are, then. It's just some kind of straight-forward deal.'

'It might be,' I agreed, 'if it wasn't for the fact that those properties were all being negotiated in Freddy's name.'

'Who told you that?'

'Someone in the Bowyers Society found out for me.'

Laurie shrugged her shoulders. 'It could be that even Freddy got involved in a legitimate deal now and again.'

'I very much doubt it.' I did, too. The chances of Freddy having done a single legitimate act in his life were about ten million to one. I said, 'A bit late to ask him now.'

'Yes.' She looked back at me bleakly. I was used to seeing Laurie doing her capable thing, but now she looked young and forlorn and vulnerable. She said, 'I suppose I ought to feel sorry for that man Wong, but I don't. He got mixed up with the Jeharis because it suited him and he must have known what would happen if he fooled around with them.'

Did he? I very much doubt if Freddy had given it a thought. Freddy had peddled unreality as a stock in trade and it simply hadn't been in his nature to look ahead. 'If you were able to ask Freddy at this moment why he did it,' I told her, 'I imagine he'd say that it seemed a good idea at the time.'

'For God's sake, Angus, it isn't *funny*!' Laurie's voice had a note in it I hadn't heard before. She said, 'Those dreadful people didn't care if they blew up any number of innocent bystanders just so long as they killed the one they wanted. It's only through sheer luck they didn't kill you.'

Luck, but not unaccountable luck, because the booby-trap can be a surprisingly sophisticated device. At its crudest, one simply links the ignition switch with the bomb, so that as soon as you start the car the thing goes off. Or you clip a relay to the door. The snag with that one is that the intended victim is still trying to get into the car when the charge is fired, which is why poor Freddy had the benefit of a relay that operated by a two-lobed cam. Two openings to one bang. The device let him in, but blew him up when he tried to get out. The passenger doors, of course, weren't triggered so if there really was any luck, it was the fact that I had been the first to get out and the explosion had literally blown me away from real harm.

Aloud I said, 'Well, the bastards didn't kill me. And anyway, it's my job.' Man's inbuilt compulsion to leap into the pit which he hath digged. I suspected as much as soon as I'd said it, but by then there wasn't much I could do about it. Not for nothing is it said that 'too late' is the saddest phrase in the English language.

'It's *not* your job! You'd never have got mixed up in this business at all if you hadn't been trying to impress bloody Angela.' Laurie stopped and sniffed. Unlike her, for she was not a sniffing woman. She said, 'Oh God, darling, I'm sorry. I'm an insensitive cow. I came to cheer you up and all I do is rave at you like a fishwife.' She gulped. 'Better go.'

'Stay,' I said.

'I don't know what for.' She looked at me in a way that was new between us. 'You don't *need* me. You have an astonishing natural talent that for once the public seem to recognize, but all you really want is to be a policeman. Oh, you're prepared to knock out the odd book from time to time because it amuses you to do the research and the money comes in useful so that you can run an expensive car, but that's it. Damn you, Angus, you don't need someone like me to guide your career because you don't want a career. All you want is to play cops and robbers and risk getting yourself killed.'

'Getting yourself killed is overrated,' I said. It was bad enough trying to talk normally with a tongue that felt twice its normal size without getting involved in an argument, and my head was tearing itself in half. I made an effort and said, 'I'm sorry.'

'It's all right.' She touched my face and her fingers were the coolest things I could remember.

I said, 'You've got my office number?'

'Yes, of course.'

'Give Sergeant Endicott a ring and tell him I want him down here tomorrow morning.'

I'd told myself I was going to feel better in the morning and I was nearly right. The pain in my head had relaxed into a kind of background throb and while no one was looking I'd discovered that so long as I thought about something else I could not only swing my legs off the bed but I could actually stand up and move around. It might not be brilliant but it was good enough. Some kind of superior nurse came in and disapproved. Not the jolly black one from my arrival but a red-haired Scots shrew.

'Mr Straun! Will you kindly get back into bed!'

I asked politely for my clothes.

'You'll no be wanting your clothes. Now into bed or I'll be calling the doctor!' She was wearing a wedding ring, I noticed, poor wee man.

'Whisht, woman!' I said. 'Get who the devil ye want. I'm signing myself out.'

She fetched a doctor, of course, and another still more senior nurse. They argued and made a fuss and in the middle of it Sergeant Endicott arrived.

'Just coming,' I told him.

He looked doubtful, full of the built-in awe in which we hold the professional classes.

'You sure you want to do this?' And then, as though it should clinch the matter, 'The Super's coming later to have a look at you.'

'You'd better get on the phone,' I told him. 'Tell him I'll come and see him.'

'Yessir. I'll do that.'

I said, 'You'd better not do it for a minute, I'll probably need you to get my clothes on.'

Forms were produced and I signed them, but getting dressed was worse than I'd expected. Standing wasn't too bad but the bending bit proved trickier. Nevertheless, it came out all right in the end, though a sight of myself in a mirror didn't help. For one thing, my suit hadn't been exactly improved by the explosion and my face looked like nothing on earth. My nose didn't matter too much because it was largely hidden by a chunk of adhesive bandage, but I hadn't reckoned on the pair of black eyes.

I asked Endicott if he'd brought a car, which was a bit late to think of, but of course he had. We walked out of the hospital together and I must admit it seemed a long way. Endicott tucked me into the passenger seat and got behind the wheel.

'The shop?'

I shook my head. 'No,' I said, 'we'll go to the Constantines' yard first.'

He looked at me doubtfully. 'Sure you wouldn't rather make it tomorrow?'

I said sharpish, 'Christ, Sergeant, if I wanted to go to-morrow—'

'—you'd have said tomorrow.' Endicott was not put out. He had, in fact, slipped into the role of male nurse pretty well. Probably he was enjoying it.

'You know where it is?'

Sergeant Endicott obviously knew where it was because he just smiled. He knew where the scrap yard was all right, because we went straight there.

The Constantines' yard was bigger than most but otherwise much of a pattern. At a guess it covered a site of about an acre, ringed around with steel mesh fencing. The only building was a largish single-storeyed shed that someone had dreamed up out of a lot of asbestos sheet and corrugated iron, the rest of the space was taken up with a bizarre collection of artefacts that someone must have collected for the sole reason that they were made of metal. Cars there were none, but I seemed to remember that cars were a different project, carried out lucratively somewhere else. But there were ancient cookers by the score, condemned washing machines in more or less orderly ranks, skylines of refrigerators, the flotsam of a thousand part-exchange deals. Ten pounds for your old cooker in any condition. On a vast pile of unidentifiable junk several men in dirty overalls climbed here and there without noticeable enthusiasm.

'Nice wheels,' Sergeant Endicott said appreciatively.

I'd noticed them too, the front end of a brand-new grey Rolls Silver Spur sticking out from behind the back of the shed. Well, the colour was an improvement on pink. I was reflecting on this when Stephanos Constantine came out of what must have passed as his office, a vision in a purple lightweight mohair suit. He gave me a long and interested look, during which I noticed that the whites of his eyes were even muddier than usual.

He said in greeting, 'Glad to see someone gave you one in the nose. Comes of sticking it into other people's business, eh?'

'I shouldn't wonder.' At least it was consistent, the front of the musical comedy crook. Was it supposed to make one discount him as a clown or was it just the way he was? All I knew about Stephanos was that he'd always been that way and I never personally found much in him to laugh at.

'So.' He scratched a silk-shirted armpit. 'What you want to ask me today?'

'Someone told me,' I said, 'that you'd gone into the car rental business. Pink Rollers for diplomats.'

All I got for that was a Greek scowl. 'You know there's no hire business. Obliged a friend, that's all.'

For some reason it hurt more to stand still than it did to

move so I went over to inspect his new car. It was restrained for its owner, but pretty nice if you liked that sort of thing. I said, 'You didn't waste much time replacing the last one.'

Stephanos made Greek movements with his hands. 'You know me, I do things quick. No hanging about. You know someone in trade, you get one off the peg. No waiting.'

'If you pay over the odds.'

An expressive shrug. 'So you pay a bit more—who cares? All legit, Inspector. On my mother's grave.' He pulled a sheet of paper from an inside pocket. 'There you go. Receipt. What's wrong with that?'

Nothing was wrong with that. The very best Mayfair dealers, dated, paid in cash. It must have shaken them rigid.

'Suppose,' I said, 'you tell me how you came to lend your last one to Freddy Wong.' I felt the twinge of a doubt. 'You did know he'd got it, I suppose?'

'He needed the car for business. Smart-looking car.' Stephanos's muddy eyes stared into mine. 'He ask if I lend him mine and I say OK. How was I to know the kind of people he was mixed up with?'

'So where did you meet Freddy Wong?'

Stephanos showed signs of impatience. 'What the hell it matter how I met him? There is no law against knowing him?' He fished in the pocket of his dreadful suit and produced a packet of cigarettes. 'OK, I met him in a pub.'

I watched a uniformed police dog-handler, complete with German Shepherd pal, pause at our car, glance towards us and then come into the yard. Stephanos had his back to him and didn't even know he was there till the PC spoke to Endicott.

'Someone on your radio's trying to raise you, Sarge.'

Endicott nodded. 'Thanks—' He broke off as Stephanos

caught sight of the dog and looked as though he'd just seen a sabre-toothed tiger.

'Out!' His voice was high. 'You have no right to bring that dog here! At once you leave!'

'Just going, mate,' the dog-handler said equably. 'No sweat.' He spoke gently to his charge and he and Endicott turned and went back to the car.

Stephanos had the grace to look sheepish. 'I hate dogs,' he said. 'Can't stand them near me.' I'd have asked him if he'd always been this way but Sergeant Endicott was trotting back.

'Call for you, sir.'

'All right.' I wondered which of my masters was going to give me a going-over for leaving hospital. Gareth Evans probably. I got into the car and picked up the handset. 'Straun here.'

It was Gareth Evans all right. Muted, though. 'Angus, where are you?'

Angus, yet. I said, 'Charlton, sir.'

'Your wife—well—Mrs Straun—' Ex-wives weren't very Chapel and I suppose I should have helped him out but I let him get on with it. Finally: 'She's on the phone. She wants to speak to you urgently.'

I said, 'Perhaps you'd ask her where she is, and I'll ring her back.'

Pause. Then Evans's voice saying, 'That won't be necessary. We can put you through.'

I felt the cold finger of unease for the first time. 'All right.'

There was another pause and a good deal of background noise. A large seagull swept in from the river, dived low over the scrap yard and alighted on the bonnet of the car, where it stared at me balefully. I didn't believe in omens but I found myself wishing hard that the damn thing would go away.

Angela's voice, high and strained. 'Angus?'

I said, 'Yes, Angie. What's the matter?'

'It's Sam,' she said. 'He's gone. Somebody's taken him away.'

CHAPTER 15

Joe Endicott would have driven me out to Hampstead but Tiverton House was on the way and I could pick up my own car there. I checked in with Gareth Evans but he knew no more than Angela had told me over the phone. That Sam had been walking the dog on the Heath, had gone off on his own while his mother had been chatting to someone she'd met, and then simply disappeared. Angela had found the dog sitting under a tree, apparently waiting for its master to come back.

'You know what kids are,' Evans said. He fiddled with his pen, avoiding my eyes. 'The little devils think it's fun to make their parents sweat. Chances are he's met some of his pals and they're hiding or something. Probably turned up by now. Hope his mother has the sense to give him a good hiding.' At six? Did one go off like that at six? I couldn't remember, but it was possible. And Evans was only doing his best, whether he believed it or not. Unfortunately, policemen are like doctors—when it comes to cheering on themselves, they know too much.

I told him how I'd spent the morning and then wrote Angela's number down. 'I'll be there if you want me.'

'Well, you can forget Wong,' Evans told me briskly. 'Terrorist Squad from now on. Glad to have him off my plate, come to that.'

I said, 'That'll please Todhunter.'

He grinned sourly. 'Strong representations the government are making. It seems the PM is tired of Islamic fundamentalism and bomb-throwing in general. Shouldn't be surprised if they're given the boot and their embassy closed down.' Evans added some kind of daisy to the flowerpot he'd been drawing and, as an afterthought, introduced a heavily striped bee. He added, 'Talking to your friend Todhunter this morning, I was. Strong he is on leaving Mr Jager alone.'

'I know,' I said. 'He made the same point to me.'

'Well, don't you forget it,' Evans told me. 'Away and find that boy of yours.'

Second tellings were something I didn't need. I went downstairs to the car park and found Sergeant Endicott standing by the Maserati, somewhat in the manner of the sentry at Pompeii.

'Anything else, sir?'

I got myself behind the wheel. Probably there was something else but I was too busy thinking about Sam to guess what it was, but I found an unexpected twinge of regret at leaving Joe behind.

'Thanks, Joe,' I said. 'Nothing else.' I reached for the key, and my eyes took in something sticking out of the parcel shelf. Usually nothing of note, just the general untidiness of maps and service manuals and the general this and that I always mean to clear up next time I get the car washed but somehow never do.

I pushed them back through force of habit but my eye caught something familiar about the top one. A bird's eye view of a kid flying a kite, the roofs of a street of houses. The printing at the top of the page read *Hallet's Panorama of Bath*. Where else had I seen that same panorama? Freddy's flat. So Freddy may have been to Bath, but I hadn't—

It fell into place. I suppose it was Sam and the bomb and the old business of the adrenalin pumping around, but what would have been odd yesterday was clear as daylight today. I said, 'Joe—'

'Sir?'

'It's Superintendent Meers on the Anti-Terrorist Squad, isn't it?' It was, I didn't have to wait for his answer. I said, 'That lighter by the Constantines' yard. Tell him to take a dog along and let it have a sniff or two.'

Joe frowned. 'Drugs?'

'No,' I said. 'Semtex.'

It didn't take me long to get to Burbeck Gardens but it made no difference, because Sam hadn't come back. Aunt Molly was out somewhere and Angela was walking to and fro inside Aspen Cottage looking like something in a zoo trying to get out. I'd gone in without knocking because the front door had been open and she'd called out to me from the living-room.

'Angus, is that you?'

I went in to her and found her staring bleakly out of the window. She'd turned and said, 'Where have you *been*?' Then I suppose she'd taken in my face. 'Darling, what on earth—?'

'It's all right,' I told her. Curiously it was all right, too. That usual comforting business of banging your head against a wall to stop your tooth hurting. I said, 'Just tell me what happened.'

She told me, in a flat monotone, what she'd told me over the phone. It was the kind of thing that happens to parents and kids all the time except that in most cases the kids come back.

'He couldn't have just vanished into thin air,' I said. 'Were there trees—people?'

Apparently there had been both. A thickish clump of trees about a hundred yards away and, at the time when Sam vanished, quite a lot of people had been in the vicinity doing the kind of thing people do on Hampstead Heath— talking, walking dogs, the adults largely ignoring the kids who yelled almost under their feet.

I asked Angela whom she'd been talking to.

She shook her head. 'I don't know who she was. A dumpy sort of woman. Fortyish, in a tweed suit.' It was like Angela to have remembered what the woman had been wearing. No, unfair. Most people retain a picture of sorts. She went on, 'You know how it is. I was standing there while Sam chased off with Toby. She was just out walking, I think. We just started talking about—I can't really remember what. The weather, I suppose.'

'Were you near a road?'

Angela nodded. 'Spaniards. There were quite a few cars parked there. They could—'

They could have taken Sam away in one of them. He could have taken him.

I said, 'Why Sam?'

Angela looked at me. 'Isn't that what everybody says?' She was sitting staring at me, her dark eyes wide, hands folded in her lap. There was a stillness about her that seemed to suggest that she'd forgotten her body, that her mind was somewhere else, with her child. She said, 'Every mother thinks it isn't going to happen to her.'

I nodded. She was right. This was every parent's hostage to fate, the unthinkable that's nevertheless always there because, like lightning, it strikes at random. Over the pain in my body I felt a clammy cold. Fear.

There's a routine for these things and I began to run through it. The local police were informed and I knew there was nothing I could add to what they would already be doing, but just going through the motions gave an illusion of getting something done.

Angela said, 'There's something I haven't told you.' I found it hard to relate to this woman I had once known so well. There had been a time when there had never been anything we weren't able to tell each other and for a moment I could have wished us back to that long-ago time again.

'All right, Angie,' I said. 'What is it?'

'I had a phone call.' She stared at me, still and remote. 'Angus, it was just before you arrived. A voice just said, *If you want the boy back, tell your husband he's working too hard. Tell him to take a holiday.*'

So the lightning hadn't struck at random after all. Whoever had taken Sam hadn't wanted just any child, they had wanted my son. I suppose I was relieved. Nobody in their right mind wants to have a child kidnapped and held to any kind of ransom, but at least I could tell myself that Sam wasn't in the hands of some sexual lunatic. I said with an effort, 'The voice. Did you recognize the voice?'

Angela shook her head. It was like a statue moving.

'Man or woman?'

'A man.' She paused. 'He sounded—odd. Disguised. As though he was speaking through a handkerchief or something.'

Well, he probably would, and disguising a voice effectively wasn't difficult. I turned away and stared out of the window. So into whose affairs was I probing uncomfortably deeply? Constantine's? Jager's? Dr Haziz? I didn't really know why I was trying to rationalize. I knew it was Jager. I couldn't pretend to know why but deep in my guts I knew that he was the man.

I said casually, 'When's your friend Jager due over here again?'

Angela stared at me as though I was mad. Well, it was understandable. At that moment her thoughts were on her child, not her boyfriend. Just the same, if I'd tried to suggest to her that there might be any connection between the two she would almost instinctively have put it down to jealousy on my part. 'For God's sake, Angus,' she said, 'what's Dirk got to do with this, anyway?'

I said, 'He's due to give evidence at Hunter's inquest

next week. I just thought he might have come over early to see you.'

'He came over early,' Angela agreed. 'But certainly not to see me. He's playing in some golf tournament on the South Coast. Lampton, I believe.' Her eyes were wide now with disbelief. 'Really, Angus, what kind of a man are you? Don't you *care* that your son's been kidnapped?' Her voice rose a fraction. 'You're a policeman, aren't you? At least, that's what you were always telling me. So why don't you do something about finding him?'

'I'm going to,' I told her. 'In the meantime you'd better stay here and do what the local police tell you.'

'Yes, but what are you going to *do*?'

'I've told you,' I said. 'I'm going to find Sam.'

Lampton was one of those hundred-year-old seaside courses that really got into their stride in the halcyon days before World War I and now soldier on, mothballed against time, ludicrously anachronistic and so sought after that a peer with a single-figure handicap can count himself lucky to get off the waiting list in less than five years. If you are coloured, Jewish, professional, female or have simply made your own couple of million, you are unlikely to get past the door of the rather scruffy-looking club house, let alone on to the highly entertaining, immaculately maintained course. *Nobody* paid a green fee unless personally introduced by a member, yet it was said that when a bar steward was accused of a particularly unsavoury crime members contributed several hundred pounds a head in order to pay for his defence—and the committee promptly sacked him on the day he was found guilty.

I rang through to Lampton from a call-box and checked that they were hosting a tournament. Yes, they were, Euro Alliance '89—an amateur competition for EEC players that had been growing in popularity over the last couple of years.

I asked if Dirk Jager was a member of the Dutch team and the answer was yes again. The second round was scheduled for the next day, first pair to tee off at eight o'clock. The girl at the end of the phone was brisk, cheerful and efficient; whoever organized things at Lampton knew his or her stuff.

I climbed back into the car and headed south.

Hampstead to Lampton is about seventy miles as the crow flies, half as much again over roads. I drove with what the official reports call due care and attention, rather slower than usual, because I hurt all over and the dressing across my nose seemed to fill half the view ahead. I took no chances, because above everything else I wanted to be sure of arriving at my destination.

An odd drive. There are always the weird ones that stick in memory, such as the one I shared with a rabid dog and the long twenty miles on a motorway with a nutter in the back seat and his gun rammed into the base of my neck. Once, years back, I'd taken the wrong kind of advice and tried to drive a jeep across a frozen river and the wheels had gone through.

Now this. In a way I was glad that my orders so clearly stated that in no way was I to make official contact with Dirk Jager, because if one is going to burn one's boats one may as well make a good job of it. And anyway, I was less interested in Jager's possible offences than the fact that I wanted Sam back.

I don't think that as I drove through Guildford and Godalming I had any fixed intention of killing Jager. It was not because I balked at the idea but simply that a dead man wasn't going to produce my son, but for virtually anything else I was ready and willing. Seen with hindsight, I was in no condition to be rational. Physically I had absorbed as much or more than I could take, and emotional stress on top of concussion is no recipe for balanced judgement. I was not, as I drove towards Lampton, wholly sane but neither was I barking mad. Simply, I was a man who knew what he meant to do, and I imagine that if I had met myself at that moment I would have got to hell out of the way.

It was seven o'clock by the time I reached Lampton and found the golf club, a couple of miles out of town. From the road in you got a panoramic view of one of the holes, a clump of trees and a low clapboard and pantiled club house just visible behind them. A couple of late players trudged in, silhouetted against the sea, and the evening light reflected off a lot of parked cars. It was the kind of scene travel firms use to advertise golfing weekends but the only effect it had on me was to make me wonder if Jager was still around. If he'd finished earlier in the afternoon he might well have gone on to his hotel. Well, if he had, no harm. One could always ask.

It was a pleasant club house, bigger than it looked from the outside, with furnishing appropriate to the carriage trade. There was some kind of reception going on in a big room with windows overlooking the course, and a near-deserted bar. I asked the white-jacketed chap behind it if there were any Dutch players about.

He said, 'You'll have to ask the Secretary.' He did not say 'sir'. Not surprising, in view of my looks, but it annoyed me at the time.

'I'm asking you,' I said. I don't suppose he knew how near he was to being savaged at that moment, because I had a desperate urge to close my hands round his throat. But discipline is the making of us. I showed him my warrant card instead.

He looked surprised, as well he might. 'Sorry, sir. But I don't know.' He caught my eye and added hastily, 'There's a tournament on. Lot of gentlemen I've never seen before.'

'Go and find me a Dutchman,' I said. 'Now.'

He went. I looked at the bottles lining the back of the bar and thought in a detached way how much I'd enjoy a drink.

My head was aching fit to bust, what was left of my nose under the strip bandage throbbed in time with my heartbeat and every time I moved my legs they sent shock waves to a brain that could barely cope anyway. Some lingering sense of caution rang an alarm bell to say no, alcohol was not a good idea, and mercifully I listened.

The steward was back with a solid-looking young man who somehow managed to look as though he was called out of parties every day by a man with a broken nose and two black eyes.

'Oh, Dirk Jager,' he said when he'd heard me out. 'He had a phone call a few minutes ago. Afraid I haven't seen him since.'

'You're very helpful,' I told him, a nice young man who was doing his best. 'You don't remember who brought him the message?'

He didn't but the steward did. All of a sudden he seemed rather pro police. In the end I found myself with the Assistant Secretary, a young woman who paid no attention to my appearance but simply answered questions. Yes, she had told the Dutch player that there was a call for him. Yes, she remembered who it was, because the caller had said to her, 'Tell him it's Sandy Smith from Thetfield.' Did the name sound right?

'Yes,' I assured her, the name was quite right. I asked, 'Were you here in the room when Mr Jager answered the phone?'

'Well—yes.'

'Obviously you couldn't hear what the caller was saying, but did you form an impression of what the call was about?' Which was pure police-speak, an insidious language if ever there was one. I enlarged. 'Did they sound—well, friendly?'

The girl shook her head. 'Not really. And, as a matter of fact, I *could* hear some of what they said. It's one of those phones—it sort of echoes.'

I made encouraging noises.

'I heard Mr Smith—the caller—say something like, "You'd better get over here right away." It must have been something like that because Mr Jager said he couldn't because he was playing a match in the morning.'

The girl was a walking recorder. I asked, 'And did you hear what Mr Smith said to that?'

'He said he didn't give—he didn't care. That Mr Jager was to come right away because he'd got Bill's radio.'

'Are you sure?'

She shook her head. 'No, not really. You know how a phone sort of squawks when it's too loud. But something like that. Anyway, it made Mr Jager very angry. He slammed the phone down and asked me if I knew the quickest way to Thetfield.'

Sandy Smith must have been really feeling his oats, I thought. But Thetfield . . . 'What did you tell him?' I asked.

The girl said, 'Well, as a matter of fact I wasn't sure but it seemed best for him to go the most straightforward way—straight up the A3 through Guildford. I showed him on a map and he went out to the car park then and there.'

'And this was what—about quarter of an hour ago?'

She nodded. 'Not more.'

Well, that was something, I supposed. Not much, but something. I said, 'Let's have a look at that map.'

She let me look and it wasn't very encouraging. The A3 was a very fair road, and I was in no shape to give that Ferrari a head start. On the other hand, Thetfield was north-west of London, which presumably meant Jager would eventually pick up the M25 orbital motorway that encircled London and travel north on it till he turned off somewhere around Rickmansworth. At this time in the evening traffic would be fairly heavy on the A3, just conceivably heavy enough to make it worth my while to drive west for an extra fifteen miles in order to pick up the motorway just above Winchester.

I thought it over. It was a long chance but I wanted to see Sandy Smith before Jager got to him. And with a quarter of an hour's start, the red Ferrari would already be at least fifteen miles ahead. I'd never overhaul that kind of lead on public roads. Stop kidding yourself, I thought, you'd never make up that distance anywhere. So I thanked the nice girl for her help and headed the Maserati towards Alresford.

After a couple of miles I stopped at a public phone-box and rang the police at Guildford. 'I don't like to make trouble for a fellow motorist, but I thought it was my duty as a citizen to inform you of this.' What with one thing and another it wasn't difficult to make my voice shake with the self-righteous venom of the professional do-gooder.

'Yes, sir?' I could see him licking his pencil.

I said petulantly, 'There's a maniac just set off up the A3 in one of those Italian cars. Ferrari? Is that right? It's red, anyway. I overheard him saying in the golf club here that he's going to try to beat his own record to London and that his car is capable of 150 m.p.h. 150 m.p.h.! Far too fast. But this chap's been in the bar for the last couple of hours—'

'He's been drinking, sir?'

I said, 'Well—frankly, yes. I think he should be stopped for his own good.'

'Yes, sir.' The voice in my ear was a good deal more interested than it had been. 'Now might I have your name, sir?'

Too late, too late. I put the phone down and got back in the car. The traffic police could hardly miss a red Ferrari, and although I very much doubted if Jager had been drinking, getting breathalysed would take a bit of time. To say nothing of having relays of patrol cars breathing down his neck every time he put his foot down. If it wouldn't have hurt my face so much, I might almost have laughed. It might not give me all that much of an edge but it would be something.

I was too far south for the homegoing London traffic to have reached me, and I started to make good time. But I was cautious as I swept through Alresford and headed for Winchester. One may chance things a little on a motorway but I had no desire to cut a swathe through Southampton's suburbia. I reached the M3, turned north and loosened the Maserati's reins a little.

At any other time I suppose I'd have enjoyed the noise of all those camshaft drives thrashing around and the slurp of the double choke Webers as they sucked in air and four star in just about equal proportions. To drive fast along a decent road should have been an experience but this night it was only a car I was steering, no more than something that would get me to my destination. I wondered what kidnappers did with their hostages if they had no accomplice. What was happening to Sam while Dirk Jager was playing golf at Lampton? Had he left the poor little devil alone in some locked room? Had he—

The car in front of me had suddenly become uncomfortably near and I skated round its back bumper with only just enough to spare, made my mind a blank. If one wants to fret about one's children, best not to do it at a hundred miles per hour. A worthy resolution but difficult. I waggled my left hand in the air and hoped the chap I'd just passed would understand.

I'd got as far as Exit 6 just north of Basingstoke before they picked me up. I'd spotted a police Rover going south on the other carriageway and there was little doubt that they'd spotted me. Full chat in a Maserati Khamsin is a hundred and fifty plus and I wasn't doing anything like that, but neither was I hanging about. I could almost hear them radioing back, so any moment now—

It came out of the slip road a quarter of a mile ahead of me, accelerating hard, blue light flashing, getting in front of me to block my path but giving me time to do something about it. An arm came out of the left-hand window and pointed to the hard shoulder. I braked, changed down and flipped in behind him. As a breaker of the law I had nothing to complain about. Slick, competent and with a minimum of hassle for all concerned.

'Good evening, sir. I wonder if you'd mind getting out of your car?' A tough, ginger-haired cop who'd done this a few hundred times and was prepared to play it by the book, if you were. I didn't get out, but gave him my warrant card.

He read it. He looked at the car.

I said, 'I'm on duty.' I wasn't, but by the time he found out it wouldn't matter. So I gave him my particulars and Gareth Evans's phone number. I added, 'And while you're at it, breathalyse me.'

'Sir?'

I said, 'For your protection, not mine.' The picture of some half-witted politician yelping in the House about policemen covering up each other's drunken revels did not appeal to me.

Ginger Whiskers nodded, not uncivil. 'If you'd blow into this, sir.'

I blew, grateful to whatever guardian shade had tapped me on the shoulder back at Lampton. Everything came up green. My chap said, 'Would you like us to give you a sort of escort, sir?'

I thanked him but shook my head. 'If you'd tell people further on.'

'I'll tell them.' He nodded cheerfully, that large comradely chap. 'Only go easy on the orbital. Too busy for larks.'

I promised no larks on the London orbital and pushed off while the going was good. I wondered how Jager was doing. If the patrols on the A3 had given him a going-over

I had a chance; if not he'd be well ahead of me by now. Well, there was nothing I could do but hope for the best, so I got on with it; the traffic was getting heavier the nearer I got to London and I made myself slow down, which was no bad thing. After more than four hours at the wheel my general wear and tear was beginning to catch up with me and I wasn't all that safe to be on the road at all, let alone trying to negotiate traffic at eighty and telling myself it was slow. Dusk was falling and I switched the lights on, then the radio. I listened to it without the slightest awareness as to what it was all about but at least it was a noise that stopped me thinking too much about Sam. A striped police car swept by in the opposite direction with its crew staring rather pointedly ahead. Happy is a man in his friends. A signpost read *Thetfield 5 miles*.

I recognized the big, fast roundabout close to the club's entrance and went in slowly, ignoring the car park and rolling to rest in the shadow of the greenkeeper's sheds. It was pretty dark now, but there was still a light here and there in the clubhouse. I had a look at the parked cars and breathed a sigh of relief at the fact that there was no Ferrari among them, so I went on towards the pro's shop. What with one thing and another it seemed a long way and I had to stop before I got to the door. Through the window I could see that Smith must have put in a lot of hard graft because the shop looked very nearly as well stocked as it had before the robbery. Smith himself was standing with his back to the door, fiddling with the training video. I went in.

'Would that be you, Jager?' He didn't turn round.

'No,' I said. 'Me.'

CHAPTER 16

Sandy Smith switched off the video and turned round. He still looked the cheeky, clean-faced young assistant pro all ready to welcome a member even if it was time to go home. But he didn't look entirely at ease.

He said, 'Sir?'

Well, I was getting used to not being recognized, so I said, 'Inspector Straun.'

'Aye. I remember.' He was staring at me as though I was something from another world, misgivings beginning to grow.

I said, 'You thought I was Dirk Jager. I'm afraid he must have got held up on the way.' It was a bit theatrical but the setting encouraged it. I went on, 'I was told you said over the phone that you had the radio, but I imagine what you really said was that you had the *video*. Why don't you put it on again?'

He went on staring at me as though he didn't know what to say and I thought he'd have got used to the idea of my being there by now. Still, surprise takes us all in different ways, and finally he said, 'I'm no understanding what you're talking about.' The lilt of Scots was more pronounced than I remembered.

'*I* didn't until just now,' I confessed. 'When I heard that you had enough clout to call Jager away from a golf tournament, I realized it must be something rather special. So switch that thing on again and let's see what it is.'

A decent enough lad, but out of his depth. He shrugged his shoulders. 'OK.' He prodded a button and the small screen lit up in truer than life colour. The picture quality was remarkably good, and I could quite see why golf pros used videos as a teaching aid, though who wants to make himself unhappy looking at his own swing? The subject on the teaching video screen was a youngish, fair-haired man who looked familiar, which wasn't surprising because as I drew nearer I could see that it was the victim of Jager's accident, Christopher Hunter. I could see Hunter full frontal, about to address the ball. At the last moment he looked up startled and spoke to someone out of frame. It startled me, too, because for some reason I hadn't expected there to be a sound track, although obviously there had to be for the teacher's voice-over.

'You mean you're serious? You're asking me to *help* you on this lunatic scheme?'

Jager's voice, instantly recognizable, came back harshly, 'It is a scheme that will work. And yes—I am asking your help.'

I watched Hunter shake his head in what can only have been disbelief. 'Then all I can say is that you're mad— bloody barking mad. I helped *design* the Thames flood barrier.'

Something dark bulked into the right-hand side of the screen and I realized I was looking over Jager's shoulder. He was saying, 'I know. That's why I need your help.' There was something slightly unnerving about the presence of that inhuman eye looking down on the two of them, but that's what the microchip does for all of us.

Hunter said, 'Well, you won't get my help. And, in any case, the whole idea is ridiculous. You can't sabotage the Thames flood barrier. The leaf gates weigh fifteen hundred tons apiece—do you think you're going to blow them apart with a pound or two of Semtex?'

The dark bulk on the right of the screen seemed to gather itself. Hunter was saying, 'Christ, I thought you were joking. You must be mad if you were taking this idea seriously. Forget it, Dirk, I'm warning you. I'll go to the police—'

The figure with its back to the camera erupted into savage movement, moving in towards the shocked figure of Hunter so that one could now recognize Jager as he swung the club he held in a long, flat backswing. There was a moment's pause and he then brought it forward again in a wristy, flailing movement that ended with a sound like an axe on wood. The clubhead of the driver caught Hunter against the side of the head and he dropped as though he'd been poleaxed. Jager leaned on his club and stared down at his body with a kind of calm. I wondered where I'd seen that sudden orgasmic rage and its curiously tranquil aftermath before. I remembered quickly enough. Jager at the 17th in Holland, winding his 9 iron round a tree.

Sandy Smith switched the video off. 'That'll be enough, I'm thinking.' The small boy caught out but keeping his end up. I wondered if he really saw himself as a master crook.

'I'm puzzled,' I said. 'Who held the camera?'

'Nobody held the camera,' Smith said. 'Bill used to hide one up in the tree overlooking the 10th tee. The idea was to take a sequence of a pupil playing sort of naturally—not *trying*, the way they do when the pro's looking on.'

I said, 'You mean it ran all day?' Not that it mattered, but it was the sort of thing I liked to find out.

'Och, it's got an interrupted beam gadget—the kind of thing used to photograph birds and so on.'

'All right,' I said, 'so Bill Tilling looked at what he'd got at the end of the day and found he'd recorded a murder. Recorded it so well he couldn't resist seeing how much the tape was worth.'

Sandy Smith nodded, the self-confident nod of the living towards the dead. He said, 'Well, you canna blame him, can you? He was on to a nice thing if he hadn't had that damn silly accident and got himself killed. But it seemed a pity to let the tape go to waste.'

As a golfer I imagined he was adequate but, God, he was thick. I said, 'You do know that blackmail is illegal, I suppose?'

He looked crafty at that. 'Anyone complained to you I've been blackmailing them?'

I sighed. 'You bloody fool, Sandy,' I said. 'Bill Tilling didn't die accidentally. He was murdered. On Jager's orders —and you'll be next. You're damn lucky I got here before he did.'

There was what people used to refer to as a pregnant pause, but a short one because something moved among the shadows at the back of the shop, then the something became a man as he stepped out into the light. It was Dirk Jager and he held a short-nosed Smith and Wesson, which was aimed rather pointedly at me.

'You didn't,' he said.

Well, it was one hell of a good entry line, and I for one wasn't going to try and take it away from him. I said, 'I must have looked in the wrong parking space.'

Jager grinned. The rather frightening self-satisfaction of the mentally different. 'Perhaps you look for the wrong car, *nietwar*? I was beginning to feel that too many people look at a Ferrari so I bring a Jaguar this time. Not a pretty car but fast.'

There had been an XJS in the car park. I reflected on the sloppy pattern of thinking that says because a man drives a certain car one day he's certain to use the same one tomorrow. Who was it said only fools have to learn by experience? Spot on, chum, whoever you were.

I said, 'Never mind the car, you bastard. Where's my son?'

Pause to contemplate me, really below proper consideration but ready to be civil. He said, 'What makes you think I know where your son is?'

'Hallet's Panorama,' I said.

I think that the chances are I really had floored him because he frowned and shook his head. 'Your crazy scheme with the Constantines,' I told him. 'To blow up the Thames flood barrier and cash in on Greenhouse One.'

Jager muttered something in Dutch and the pistol swung up slightly, which reminded me that unstable people are dangerous enough armed without consciously trying to provoke them. But in for a penny, in for a pound. I said, 'Anyone can go and tour the flood barrier. Your ticket also let you in to see a panorama of Bath, painted by a chap called Hallet. God knows what it's got to do with the Thames, but there it is.'

'So?'

'So Freddy Wong must have had a look at the place on your behalf because I saw his leaflet for the panorama when I went over his flat, although it didn't ring a bell with me at the time. But there was another one in my car, left over from when I took my boy to the same place a couple of months ago. My guess is that you thought—'

'To hell with what you thought.' Jager held out his hand to Sandy Smith. 'Give me that tape.'

I told myself that if I'd been in better shape I could have jumped him, but I doubt it. Jumping a man with a gun in his hand and which he doesn't mind using is a fringe sport, with little future in it. At that moment I wanted Jager dead, but I could hardly stand, let alone cover the fifteen feet or so between us before he pulled the trigger, and at that range he could hardly miss.

'The tape!' He was getting impatient.

Sandy Smith ejected the cassette. He said slowly, 'Did ye really have Bill killed?'

Jager said, 'Yes. You too if you do not hurry up.'

I saw Winnie Tilling come in and stand in the open door behind him, and my first impulse was to shout to her to go

away, but something told me to keep quiet. She was in
shadow so it wasn't easy to see her clearly, and I had to
have a second look before I realized that she was holding a
couple of rabbits in her left hand, and perhaps half a second
more to work out what she would probably be holding in
her right. Too late.

'*Did ye have him killed?*'

'*Yes—*'

'You bastard!' Winnie said. There was a soft thump as
she dropped the rabbits and swung up the Winchester.
Jager was turning, but by that time Bill Tilling's widow had
shot him once in the back and was pumping a second round
up the spout.

If you hit him in the right place you can kill a man pretty
efficiently with a .22 but it doesn't exactly have the stopping
power of a Magnum. Jager went on turning and it seemed
to take for ever. Had I been armed I could have drawn and
fired in the time, but that would have been a foreign and
unsporting trick. Better by far that ten policemen have their
heads blown off than that the hair of a single villain be
disarranged. I took the cassette from Sandy Smith's hand
and spun it at Jager's head.

'You bastard! You bastard!' Winnie was sobbing as she
raised the rifle again. She was just too slow. The cassette
I'd thrown hit Jager just under the ear with a high plastic
clatter but he fired just the same and Winnie went over like
one of her own rabbits. He didn't fire again. He didn't even
look behind but went forward at a kind of stumbling run,
past the woman's body on the floor and out through the
door beyond.

'God!' Sandy Smith said. 'Oh God! Winnie!'

We went over to her. Jager had reeled out of the door,
one hand clutched against his body, where the little slug
had presumably lodged and where I hoped it was giving
him hell.

To Sandy Smith I said, 'Get the light on.'

It was reassuring. Either she'd fainted or the impact of the .38 bullet had knocked her out, either way Winnie was unconscious with blood beginning to well from a hole in her shoulder. I breathed a sigh of relief that it was the kind of wound that, had she been in a Western, would have healed nicely by the end of the second reel. Sandy Smith was fussing over her like an old hen. I picked up the Winchester and went out to look for Jager.

It was cool outside and the drone of the traffic on the busy road outside the gates seemed a long way away. I could hear stumbling footsteps crossing the car park ahead of me.

I shouted, 'Stop!'

A car door slammed and the engine of the Jaguar burst into life. Back tyres spun on the gravel as Jager slammed the coupé into reverse and roared towards me. I fired twice at the big tyres but with what result I had no idea.

Shoot-out in golf club.

Just great for the Sunday tabloids, I thought. I stumbled towards the Maserati as the Jaguar swung out into the exit driveway and accelerated hard. For some reason I just stood there and watched the big car as it stood for a moment silhouetted against the lights from the road beyond. Then it swung right, the tyres squealed and it was gone. Right. *Right?*

I heard the sudden wild screech of brakes, someone blasting a useless protest on the horn and then an appalling, metal-rending crunch that seemed to go on for ever.

CHAPTER 17

'So he turned right instead of left,' I said. 'Why not? If you're on the run with a bullet in you, instinct takes over, and—for a Dutchman—instinct says you drive on the right, not the left. I'm just glad he drove into a forty-ton truck. At least that way he only hurt himself.'

Laurie put coffee beside me on the bedside table. She was wearing a white towelling bathrobe and her fair hair spilled over her shoulders like a TV ad for somebody's shampoo. With her huge glasses perched on her nose, she looked as scrubbed and healthy as a schoolgirl who'd got up early to finish her homework. And sexy with it. She asked, 'And he's still alive?'

'He was when they got him to hospital last night.' And a long night it had been. Jager to hospital. Winnie to hospital. The local force called in and a statement from Sandy Smith. I wondered what instinct for survival had steered me clear of the bachelor heaven of Hallam Mews and deposited me on Laurie's doorstep. Well, hardly just instinct for survival. She was my girl and I felt like the wrath of God, so where else?

Laurie sat on the edge of the bed and sipped her own coffee. 'You slept like a log. How do you feel?'

'Stiff.' The great British understatement. I knew that in theory I'd move again but at this moment it took some believing.

She said, 'I'm not surprised. Have you *seen* yourself in a mirror?'

I hadn't actually. 'Tell me.'

'You're black and blue.'

'I feel black and blue.'

'I mean literally. You were mad to have left hospital.' Laurie bit her lip. 'All right, I won't go on about it again. But can't you take it easy today?'

I looked at her.

'OK, so you've got to find Sam. But you're in no state to go rushing around yourself. Be reasonable.' She was not a girl given to pleading.

I hauled myself upright. 'So what do you suggest I do? Stay at home and look at TV?' Of course I knew the answer to that one. My place was with Angela, even though as soon as she saw me she would yell at me to go and find Sam and I would agree with her.

Laurie and I looked at each other. There were times when I knew she could read my mind and this was one of them. She said at last, 'Look, you'd better go and see Angela. You can't just leave her there staring out of the window and waiting for someone to ring her. At least you can tell her how the hunt is getting on. You can tell her something—'

She went on talking but I wasn't listening to her. Why is it that it can take so long for the obvious to become clear? I didn't know, but as I got out of bed I did know what it was that had been hiding somewhere at the back of my memory these past few days.

'Now what?' Laurie was demanding.

I said, 'I can't stay here. Got to go somewhere.'

'Go where, for God's sake?'

I held her briefly. It was difficult to let her go. I said, 'Look, it's a hunch. If I talk about it, it'll go away.' It wouldn't. The truth was I just didn't want to talk about it. But I owed her. I said, 'That bit about Angela staring out of the window. That's exactly what she was doing when she told me about Sam.'

Laurie frowned. 'It's a natural enough thing for her to do, so?'

I said, 'So I was married to her for eight years. I know what she's like under stress, and that isn't the way she reacts. When Angela is really worried she fiddles. Tears up bits of paper. Ties knots in handkerchiefs—that kind of thing. Angela's never sat still in her life. Sitting staring at nothing is what she *thinks* people do when their heart is breaking. She probably read it in a book.'

We looked at each other. Finally Laurie said, 'Where?'

I said, 'I'll tell you when I'm sure. But this time I think I'd better go alone.'

I drove up the A1 until just before Peterborough and then turned east through the fen country to Guyhirn and on again to Wisbech. It's a strange country, the land of the fens, a grey world as flat as your hand, an endless vista of huge fields and deep-cut drainage dykes with roads that run beside them as straight as an arrow for mile after mile. Here and there one comes to a tiny haggle of houses but they have an air of being deserted, whether they are or not. There is a strange feeling of hostility about the land, as though it resents people. A spooky place, redolent of some old evil, but as the light changes under the wide sky, not without a beauty of its own.

I was having to map-read by now, but eventually I hit Long Sutton and into the lost land between its single, endless street and the line of the Wash. It was a trip that took me a good three hours but in the end there was a signpost to Sedge End. Sedge End was where Joan and Susan Anstey lived, Angela's friends from schooldays. I'd only met them once but I'd liked them well enough. 'You trust your school-friends,' Angela had once said. 'Schoolfriends never let you down.' Nice, remote schoolfriends let you down even less.

After a couple of miles I found a sail-less mill painted with pitch, black against the sky, and I knew I'd arrived. There was a fenced-off paddock which was home to a fat white pony, which, as I drove up, was being fed carrots by a small boy. I got out and leaned on the fence and tried to smile.

I got a wave and a smile and a quick scurry of small legs in my direction. 'Hi, Dad!' said Sam. 'Mum didn't say you'd be coming.'

'She must have forgotten,' I said.

I left Sam with the Ansteys, a nice couple who pretty obviously hadn't any idea that they were doing anything other than look after the boy because—as they told me cheerfully—Angie was away in London hunting up a job. Sam was blissfully happy there, learning to ride the pony, and one of the Anstey women, whom he called 'Aunt Susan', seemed to enjoy teaching him. It would have been cruel to tell any of them that they were being conned, so I had a cup of coffee with them and left them to it. Sam was dutifully concerned about my face but I told him I'd walked into something and he was quite satisfied. If you looked at it that way, I'd conned him too.

I went back to London by way of Hampstead. My one-time wife was in the garden doing things to roses, and I suppose she could tell by the way I looked that the game was up.

'Why did you do it, Angie?' I asked her civilly enough. When the penny had first dropped and I'd realized the whole kidnap story was as phoney as hell I could cheerfully have killed her, but most murder is done in hot blood and mine was cold by now.

She started to cry. There are times when a woman's tears can be effective but this wasn't one of them and I shut her up, sharpish. Finally she said, 'Dirk asked me to.'

'Christ!' I said. I took the secateurs out of her hand because she was going snip-snip-snip in the air. I said, 'You stashed my son away in the back of beyond and then told me he'd been kidnapped. You let me imagine all the things happening to him that we know do happen to children in this country. You're not a fool, so you must have known exactly what you were doing. You put me through hell and you did it because your lunatic Dutch lover *asked* you to.' I realized I was shouting.

Angela sniffed. 'He's not a lunatic.'

Eight years, I thought. Eight years we had lived together as man and wife. I realized that I wanted to hurt her physically and I got a hold on myself as I said, 'Do you know *why* he needed to put the screw on me?'

'He said he had an important deal on and you were making things impossibly difficult for him just because of an accident.' Angela had taken off her garden gloves and was busy straightening the fingers that were already straight. Fiddle fiddle fiddle. Oh, she was worried about Dirk all right. She said, 'There was something on the news this morning about him. It said he'd been taken to hospital after a road accident.'

'Yes,' I told her. 'He has.'

'I tried to find out from the hospital how he was but they wouldn't tell me.'

'That's normal,' I said. 'He's under police supervision.'

'But *why*?'

I said, 'Well, for a start, your precious Dirk didn't kill Christopher Hunter by accident. He murdered him quite intentionally in one of his nasty fits of temper.'

'You're jealous,' Angela said. She stopped fiddling with one glove and started on the other. 'Why on earth should Dirk kill his golf partner?'

'For the same reason he had the Constantines fix Freddy Wong,' I told her. 'A murderous temper and a conviction he was being betrayed by someone he trusted. Jager employed Christopher Hunter as his technical adviser on Thames flooding, and he trusted him because they were distantly related. I got my assistant to check back on the family and it seems Hunter's branch of it settled over here generations ago. That was when they Anglicized the Dutch "Jager" to its British equivalent, "Hunter".' Angela just stared at me. Perhaps, I thought, it's taken all this time for me to realize that she's beautiful but not very bright, and suddenly it became rather important to make her understand. 'Listen,' I said, 'you were right about Freddy being a con man. He showed Jager a forged official document on the greenhouse effect on the Thames and tried to make him invest money on the strength of it.'

'I knew that Chinaman was no good,' Angela said. 'I told you. And Dirk was so trusting.'

'Dirk Jager was about as trusting as a shark,' I said. 'He was a natural crook into the bargain and, like his father, slightly mad. He was so taken with Wong's scheme that he decided to improve on it by sabotaging the Thames flood barrier at the time of the highest tide. In the meantime he'd got Wong to buy options on millions of pounds' worth of office property on ground that was high enough to be safe from flooding. He reckoned useable office property would be at a premium in a flooded London and he'd make the financial killing of all time.'

Angela looked thoughtful. 'Well, I suppose he would have done, wouldn't he?' She was so besotted that she was still convinced that anything Jager had done was clever.

'No,' I told her, 'it would never have worked. Greenhouse One was a forgery, so there was never going to be a flood. It is physically impossible to sabotage all seven gates of the flood barrier with anything short of a nuclear warhead. And if by some unbelievable chance London really was flooded to that extent, the properties Wong had chosen would have been concrete islands in the middle of a sea, powerless, lightless and approachable only by boat.'

'Don't be absurd, Angus,' Angela said. 'Dirk would have seen through a scheme as wild as that.'

I said wearily, 'Con men and their targets aren't like other people. It's a private world of twosomes that outsiders can never understand. Technically, I know what they do and how they do it. I know that essentially Jager believed Wong's lunatic story because he wanted to believe it—and that Wong was a master con man because he knew exactly the level of fantasy that would be irresistible. I know this,' I said, 'but I don't understand it.'

There was more to it than that, I thought. With someone like Freddy Wong I suspected there was the thrill of the chase that would be half the fun. With Freddy there had been a compulsion to exercise his craft, enough was never enough. He'd tried it on me, he'd actually tried it on that bunch of assassins in the Jeharian Embassy, which was a kamikaze flight of fancy if ever there was one. And finally he'd tried it once too often on Jager.

Angela said softly, 'I'm sorry I hurt you, Angus. But I love Dirk so much. I'd do anything for him.'

'Yes,' I said, 'I'd noticed that.'

'I don't know what to do now.'

She looked at me. I looked at her. Nothing. I felt absolutely nothing. 'Well,' I said, 'you could always send him some flowers.'

'They found Semtex on the Constantines' lighter,' Gareth Evans Superintendent was saying. 'Bomb Squad have identified it in what was left of the Rolls, too.'

I said, 'A few pounds of Semtex wouldn't have gone far with the flood barrier.'

'They were going to blow up the lighter as it crossed the barrier,' Evans explained. 'Sink it on top of the underwater gate, see?'

'Stephanos is talking, then?'

'Like a dream. Seems Jager hired him to make a clean sweep of the golf shop so nobody would have a hint of what he was really after. Pointless, because the tape was safely up a tree all the time.' My master broke off. 'All right, boyo, why were you so sure it was the Constantines and not the fundamentalist mob who blew the Rolls? It was Stephanos's pride and joy, that pink job.'

'He'd got a new one,' I explained. 'I think Jager bought it for him as payment for blowing up his beloved pink job along with Freddy. I know Stephanos told me a yarn about insurance money but that was just another Greek fairy tale.'

Evans looked critical. 'What makes you so sure?'

I said, 'Stephanos showed me the invoice for the new Rolls. It was dated the day *before* Freddy had his little accident.'

'And the Semtex? How did you know it was there?'

It would have been easy to say it was a hunch but it had been more than that—the juxtaposition of a couple of facts that together happened to have set the alarm bells ringing. I said, 'When I went over to Freddy Wong's apartment he'd got a lot of books on the raid on Zeebrugge in World War I, which seemed curious reading for the kind of man he was. Then, while I was talking to Stephanos, a police dog-handler dropped by and the Greek got very edgy. Said he hated dogs, which was a lie, because his wife has one. But when I put together the Rolls blowing up and the fact that the Zeebrugge raid featured the blocking of a waterway with a ship loaded with explosives I couldn't help feeling that Stephanos's reaction had nothing to do with disliking dogs. He just knew that sniffer dogs are used to detect explosives.' I thought that over and added, 'It wouldn't have worked anyway. The Zeebrugge act. No use sinking a lighter to cripple one barrage gate when there are seven of the things.'

Gareth Evans smiled. 'If you can sell the Eiffel Tower twice in one day without anyone asking who's selling it—relax, bach. They don't think like us.'

'So what,' Laurie asked, 'is going to happen to Sam?'

We were eating out. I was on sick leave, on call for evidence and so on, but leave just the same. I said, 'Sam will go on just as before. The only difference will be that in future when I take him out I do not see Angela.'

'Do I gather,' Laurie said, 'that Angela has irrevocably blotted her copybook?' She stopped. 'Sorry. That was a childish thing to say.'

That odd, lingering hold that Angela had kept over me.

I thought I'd kept it to myself but it was obvious that Laurie
had known about it all along. I wondered if I should try to
explain that the break was final at last but decided that it
wasn't necessary because she obviously knew anyway. But
there were things—one thing—to be said, and it was time
I said it. I looked across the table and wondered why I'd
waited so long, and at the same moment the waiter leaned
across from behind me and murmured that I was wanted
on the telephone.

Gareth Evans, who else? 'I thought you'd be wanting to
know. The hospital phoned to say Jager died half an hour
ago.'

I thought that over. What would happen to Jager's hold-
ings in the Middle East consortium that the Foreign Office
set such store by? I hadn't the faintest idea.

'Well,' I said, 'I suppose it saves a lot of trouble.'

There was a pause, and the line clicked for a bit and a
very faint and unknown voice said, 'Tuesday night, then,
definite—'

'I don't know about that, boyo,' Gareth Evans was saying
in my ear. 'The Foreign Office won't like this. They won't
like it at all . . .'